HOOKED ON A CALIFORNIA KINGPIN 2

A BBW ARRANGED MARRIAGE

MASTERPIECE

❀ Created with Vellum

SUBSCRIBE

Interested in keeping up with more releases from S.Yvonne Presents? To be notified first on upcoming releases, exclusive sneak peaks, and contest to win prizes. Please subscribe to her mailing list by texting Syvonnepresents to 22828

SYNOPSIS

Synopsis

The finale has arrived and is packed with action, love, and even more betrayal!!! What started as an arranged marriage has become something more than what Sovereign or Malice thought it could ever be. Learning more about each other while Sovereign has a list of people that she never thought would stab her in the back can be more challenging than anything one could imagine. Her father is back in the picture and Sovereign becomes more conflicted since she was left as a young teen to provide for herself. Boundaries are crossed, lessons are learned, relationships that were built off love will end permanently! Find out what happens in the last installment of Hooked On A California Kingpin.

STAY CONNECTED

Contact the author!
Hey Pieces! It means so much to me to get your honest feedback. Please feel free to join my private readers group on Facebook! **Masterpiece Readers**
Join my mailing list by texting **Masterpiecebooks** altogether to the number 22828!
Contact me on any of my social media handles as well!
Facebook- Authoress Masterpiece & Masterpiece Reads
Facebook private group for updates- Masterpiece Readers
Instagram- authoress_masterpiece & masterpiece_lgee
Email – masterpiece3541@outlook.com

RECAP

RECAP
Sovereign

I sat at the dinner table ignoring all the praise I had received from the meeting. Everyone seemed pleased with my actions except my bitch ass husband. Malice was really starting to become a nightmare for me. This whole marriage had me feeling like I was living in some twilight zone. It felt like he was trying to force cuffs on me and keep me as his personal prisoner. One thing I couldn't deny was how each time he eyed me, he caressed every part of my body. Sexually he was the best I ever had, he overpowered my body and had the magic key to make me say and do crazy shit in bed. My body caved in and bowed down to him every time. My mind always wanted the opposite.

"Eat your food, Sovereign." He looked at me from across the table, sitting his fork down. His rough deep voice sent tremors down my spine. Always demanding, always telling me what to do like I was a child of his. I was tired of Mexican food. It's all we ever ate day and night. I was ready to get

back to the city. I needed to desperately get back to my sister. I needed to look her in the eyes and get some understanding. She was a part of me, if this was betrayal then she would be the third person to step all over my heart. A painful lump formed in my throat just thinking about my Empress. I was falling into a deep pit of depression, and I didn't know how to stop it.

I tried to force my armor of being strong to hide how I was feeling. Slowly but surely, I felt myself cracking into small pieces. Picking up my spoon I scooped up some rice and beans and placed the combination in my mouth. I tuned them out until Roberto looked at me and smiled. His aura seemed to lighten my mood, so I smiled back.

"You want kids with my hermano, Chica?" He put the taquito between his index finger and thumb like it was a blunt and fake puffed from it before taking a bite.

"No, I don't. Kids will get in the way of business." I followed up, not wanting to reveal that I couldn't have kids. At least I thought I couldn't. If I could have kids, I'd never have them with a crazy muthafucca like his brother. I was plotting a way to get away from him when I made it back to the states. Once I saw Empress' condition, I would take her away from Malice's people.

"Kids can be taken care of by di grandparents." My Abuela smiled as she picked up her cup and sipped. I ignored her and played around with my food. I could feel Malice's eyes on me, and I ignored his stare. For years, I felt numb when it came to the opposite sex. The only thing I used a nigga for was sex and half the time that wasn't satisfying enough. The twins definitely pleased me by licking and sucking all over me, but they didn't compare to Inferno. Not even their average size dicks compared. Inferno's dick was bigger than both of their dicks put together. The length and

size, the way he stroked inside of me and touched me had me wet every time he was near.

I never gave a damn about who a nigga was laying pipe too either until I stumbled on this dick head. He was to intense, too cocky, he knew how he operated in the bedroom. I hated him for trying to wake something up inside of me that I buried a long time ago with Melvin.

"Hermano." (Brother) Roberto smiled and popped his cherry red lips. He stood up from the table and moved his imaginary bang from in front of his face. Roberto was so damn random, but I loved his randomness, while we sat at a table full of serious individuals Roberto was the one to lighten up the mood.

"Not now, Roberto. The adults are talking." He winked making me roll my eyes hard at him.

"I just want to say something really important since everybody's so serrrriiioousss." He stood up and put his hand on his hip.

"I'm not gay no more...I am DELIVERT! I likes women." He dropped down low and popped his ass before standing back up. "I saiiiiddddd! I'm not gay no more! I like womenssss! Women! Women! Women!" He switched his hips and cat walked around the huge dinner table until he was standing behind me.

"Like Andrew Caldwell said. I am delivveeerttttt!" He kissed me on the forehead then cheek, placing his arms around my neck he hugged me from behind. I couldn't hold my laugh; I started cracking up. The look on Malice face was comical. His brown skin turned red, even their father started to chuckle.

"Wheeewww, I saw that on TikTok honey. Y'all was starting to suffocate me with all this masculine dead energy." He fanned himself then stuffed his mouth with food. I found

myself relaxing a tad bit. I still had a mission to go on at midnight. Murder was on my mind; I didn't give a damn about anything else but handling what my Abuela sent me to go do so then I could check up on my sister.

Excusing myself from the table, I went to Inferno's private study room where he was starting a new book collection. Pulling out my phone, I called the only person that I knew to keep it real with me.

"How are you, Queen?" His deep voice held skepticism in it. If anybody stayed worried for me, it was Bundy.

"I'm worried, Bundy. How is she?" I took a seat behind the oak wood desk and placed Bundy on speaker.

"She's fine, not talking or making eye contact with anyone but she's fine. She has asked for you, said she needs to speak to you about somethings."

"I understand." I got quiet wishing I had a blunt and a glass of Dusse. I desperately needed something to calm down my anxiety.

"Teddy has been moving the same. I can see the worry in his eyes. You do understand that the kid was just protecting his household, right?" I could hear Bundy's heavy breathing; I nodded my head instinctively like he could see me. I had to pay Teddy a visit. I didn't want him to think that I was now against him. I understood that Empress was on some sneaky weird shit. Teddy killing Murk'um and shooting Empress was what Teddy was supposed to do. I was only human and couldn't help but to worry about Empress. It had been me and her when there was nobody else.

"I understand, let him know that it's all love and I'll see him soon." I tapped my fingers against the desk.

"Got you, Queen. I miss you, want you to be safe. Who been rolling up your blunts since you not around me?" I bowed my head and smiled, licking my lips I softly laughed.

Bundy got on my nerves because he never hid the way he felt about me. He was a good friend and always made sure my needs were met, even if they were the smallest things.

"She has been rolling them herself, because she chooses to." Inferno stepped into the small dimly lit room. Flicking his lighter torch on and off. I pressed the end button on the call and looked into his eyes.

"Seems like he might be a problem that my flamethrower will solve." He walked around the desk right into my space. He sat at the edge of the desk and kept his eyes locked with mine.

"Bundy is my business." I didn't blink, I just kept my gaze locked with his.

"My wife business is my business." He smiled, leaning forward to stroke my left cheek. I hated the instant goosebumps that covered my skin just from one simple touch from him.

"You're sadly mistaken Malice, now if you will excuse me. I have to prepare for a late-night mission." I stood to my feet and prepared myself to walk away, until he grabbed me firmly by the wrist.

"I don't think you understand, Sovereign. The pussy is remarkable as fuck, it proceeds itself and speaks loud as fuck to me. It's so good that from now on, if I even think a nigga is fondling it or even fantasizing about feeling you then his flesh will burn slowly, until I have a niggas skeleton bone in Hades." He yanked me between his legs and grabbed a handful of my ass, giving a tight firm squeeze, I simpered and closed my eyes briefly.

"You got a good mouthpiece on you. I can't wait to see the way these soft pretty plump lips feel like on the tip of my dick. That tongue spit fire and I know when it strokes that sensitive vein on the shaft of my dick, I'll release down your

virgin feeling throat. You're all mine Sovereign, you're a Ruiz. A Queenpin, you will learn your rightful place as my wife and the respect will follow." He released the grip he had on my ass and smacked my ass hard; the sting had my clit thumping hard.

"Now run along... Do this last mission for your Abuella, so all of her skeletons can fall out of her closet. Daddy will be here to clean up another mess of yours." He stood off the desk, forcing me to take a couple of steps back from him. Grabbing my chin, Malice leaned down to kiss me and I turned my head letting the kiss land on my cheek. Squeezing my chin tight, he chuckled and walked away.

"Four men will accompany you tonight. My men, not your Abuella's. Enjoy tonight, this will be the last time you get your hands dirty. We are too wealthy for such things. It is an insult to me, to have my wife doing peasant kind of work." Closing the door behind him, I stood in the same spot for ten minutes straight. Shaking off the weird eerie feeling that formed into the pit of my stomach, I walked out of the room to go to our master suite to suit up for tonight's events.

"Remember, Sovereign... give them headshots. Nothing to be explained, in and out." My Abuela sat up in bed with her nightly glass of wine. I don't know why I traveled here first; she insisted that I came to see her before carrying out the hit she put me on.

"I hear you, Abuela." I gave a small smile. I hadn't told her about what all was going on back in the states. Tomorrow, I planned on explaining to her what all took place with her favorite grandchild.

"You make me so proud, El amado." (Beloved) she smiled and coughed a little. "I just wish, you Papa could see what all he could have been. Surely, he lives through you." My heart ached at her revelation. I learned a long time ago to

just let my Abuela talk. Elders were stuck in their own beliefs. I didn't like wasting time and energy trying to convince her of my own beliefs. I hated when she mentioned my father. She never acknowledged my mother unless she had something bad to say.

"When you see me tomorrow, we will talk about this Melvin... and his whereabouts." That brought me joy. I was ready to carry out this hit just to get a step closer to my own revenge. I leaned forward and placed a kiss on my Abuela's cheek. There was nothing left to say.

The city of Mexico seemed to never sleep. I loved the architecture of the entire country. Some parts were dirty and gritty, while other parts seemed magical. I thought back to how my father used to reminisce about being here and I remembered the pride he took in his country.

"I always know I'm home Mijo by the smell of fresh tortillas. It's all about life's simple pleasures." My father was a simple man; it never took too much to make him happy. I loved my mother the same but because of me being a daddy's girl, I missed him more.

Just like my Abuela said the city Pueblos Ma'gicos was lit up and looked very magical. Instead of trash being littered around on the streets, it was clean. No kids out roaming the streets. Everyone seemed to be in their homes sleeping. This was like the Beverly Hills of Mexico. It was one way in and one way out, making the escape more dangerous.

"Park around back, I don't need you all going in with me. I want to be in and out, no hiccups." I didn't like doing dirt with people. I didn't have time to be worried about the moves the other men made. Plus, I didn't feel comfortable with them. I didn't trust these niggas with my life.

"Don't get out this car, I don't need attention on us either." We were about an hour in a half away from Malice's

place. I had no plans of even going right back to his house either. I was going to spend the night at my Abuela's and then take the private jet back to Cali in the morning.

Hopping out so I wouldn't hear them protesting to me making them stay in the car. The cold crisp air hit my face first, I threw my black hoodie over my head and glanced down at my rose gold Patek. It was nearing one in the morning. This couple was old, so I was sure that they had to be sleep. Checking my surroundings, I saw nothing out of the ordinary. My Maxim Nine Mili gun cost a grip. It was the world's first integrally suppressed nine-millimeter handgun. I didn't need to connect a silencer to it. I imagined the cost but didn't know because my Abuela gave it to me as a gift.

Walking through the backyard, I admired the rose bed the married couple had leading up to the back door. My conscience told me something wasn't right when the back door unlocked and opened with no problem. The smell of fresh tortillas hit my nose first along with spices. The house was traditionally crafted out of stone walls and archways with low ceilings. I walked so softly that I couldn't hear my own footsteps. The palms of my hands started to sweat from anticipation. It was different killing someone that had wronged me. I never killed for others especially not knowing why the fuck I was even killing.

My Abuela wanted me to shoot on sight. Hopefully they were tucked in bed sleep. The front room was dark, but the moonlight shone through.

"I've waited for you for over a decade. I purposely leave the front and back door open for Ju. Turn the light on and show me your pretty face Sovereign." That weakened voice came from a rocking chair that faced the window. His dry vocal cords sounded stringy and strained. I had the perfect opportunity to kill him now and find his wife. I couldn't do *that because this old ass man called me by my government and not too many people had the pleasure of knowing that. Curiosity coursed through me as I squinted to find the light switch.*

Once the light came on, I quickly walked around until I came face to face with a wrinkly old man that looked like he was in his late eighties.

"We don't have much time Sovereign." My hands started to shake as I licked my lips.

"Time for what?" I gritted placing my index finger on the trigger.

"My execution. My little sister is very powerful and persistent. She sent you here to kill me and my wife." My stomach tightened and a million questions roamed through my mind. If Abuela would kill her own brother, who else would she kill.

"Tio?" (Uncle) that voice instantly brought tears to my eyes. My skin became clammy, and I started to sweat profusely even though the house was cold. I hadn't seen that face since I was a kid, but I'd never forget that thick accent and deep voice.

"Who are you in here talking to?" My breathing became shallow as I attempted to speak but nothing came out. I was starting to become overwhelmed with a million emotions as the footsteps down the dark hallway came closer.

I saw his face first, and we both remained stuck in place as if time stood still.

"We don't have much time, Mijo." I heard this crazy old man talking but my eyes were currently locked in with my...

"Papa?" I said a little above a whisper before everything started to spin around me. My vision blurry, I felt myself hitting the cold tile floor before darkness consumed me.

MELVIN

$\mathcal{M}$y fingers tapped against the windowpane. I watched the breeze from outside rustle the big trees from the mountaintops as waves crashed against the sharp deadly rocks beneath the house. This bitch was living like a real-life Queen. She didn't deserve any of this shit.

"YOU GOT to play shit cool son. You know how ugly this can get." I turned away from the windowpane giving my father my full attention. He laid comfortably in the bed next to Miguella like he was finally happy to get to his old wrinkled-up bitch.

"PLAY WHAT COOL?" I asked calmly as my eyes focused on Miguella. I could see the fear that radiated off of her as she gripped my father's hand tighter. See, everyone feared this bitch, but if it was someone she feared… that person would be me. It was nothing for me to push my authority down a bitch's throat hard and forcefully until they got the fucking picture on who ran shit.

THE ONLY FEMALE that I never raised my fist to was Queen, she was a different breed. It's why I fell for her and still was stuck on her. Sovereign's whole aura was powerful even if she didn't realize it or not. No man could break a bitch like Sovereign down. She let the streets groom and raise her. She could sense and feel things without you telling her what the deal was. I missed her like crazy and I wished I never fell down the rabbit's hole with my father and Miguella.

I CAN'T BLAME Miguella a hundred percent for this, because she warned me to never fall for her granddaughter. It was easy at first until I really got to know Sovereign. When I first realized that my feelings for her were growing a little too strong, I started fucking on Empress. I never felt shit for Empress. I just always saw her as an easy plan B. Empress was easy as hell to persuade then and now. It's just back in the day when she was much younger, she was easier to mold and guide.

Empress took my word and believed anything I said without a reasonable doubt.

"It seems like I'm the only one that's losing in this whole situation. You two, are really cozy, you rich as fuck because of the sugar momma that's laying so conveniently next to you. What the fuck do I have?!" My voice raised a couple of octaves. I watched the uncomfortable looks take over their faces as I moved closer to where they laid. I never wanted to come back to Mexico. With Empress missing in action and no one reaching out and letting me know what the fuck was going on with Sovereign, I decided to take a trip with my father.

MONEY WAS BACK RUNNING LOW, my expenses were high, including all the bills and the kind of lifestyle I lived. I was never giving up my expensive lifestyle. I deserved the shit after all these two had me going through.

EVERY COUPLE OF MONTHS, my father would come out to Mexico to lay up with Miguella. She took good care of him. My poor mother thought that her husband was out on business while he was really laid up with his side bitch. As old as Miguella was, my father was madly in love with her and would jump at anything she said. It's why I was in the situation that I was in now. Watching my fucking back wherever I went.

EVERYBODY GOT to tell their side of the story in part one. Now it's my turn to have some say so in this shit, to let you one sided folks know how all this shit even came about.

"SOVEREIGN IS WRAPPED up in grief, she won't come after you. She's too worried about the betrayal of Empress. After I sent Sovereign to kill my brother and his wife, she said she needed time to think and to see about Empress. She got shot trying to rob her own sister." She stopped talking and let out a soft laugh followed by a rough cough.

. . .

"Go live life and thrive. It's time you let my granddaughters go Melvin." She coughed a little more, grabbing her chest like it pained her. My father hopped up to his feet and left the room, leaving Miguella and I alone. His pitiful ass was about to go fetch her ass some wine or water.

"Should I let you go too, Miguella?" I stepped closer to her side of the bed and leaned down a little. "What would my father think of you? If only he knew how much you loved this dick of mine more than his." She pushed the covers up to her chest and looked at me as if she was seeing a ghost.

"Wire two million to my account and I better have it in twenty-four hours. If I don't then the granddaughter that I really want will have to see me soon. Maybe it's time for her to know how treacherous her sweet old abuela is." I smiled and turned to walk out. I was stopped dead in my tracks when she spoke.

"You have always been a cheap degenerate, especially to higher civilization." She cleared her throat and sat up in bed.

"I don't care what Sovereign finds out, so you can't hold anything substantial against me like you do Empress. However, I will send you ten million to disappear and stay the fuck away from Sovereign and I. Our business is done, if you were to speak any of this to Sovereign. She already knows deep down that there is no way out of the cartel. The only thing that will change is her outlook on me. I don't want her

4

respect wavering for me. Now when I die that's something different." She stared off for a couple of seconds like she was actually thinking.

"THE TEN MILLION is for no bad blood, Melvin. Let it all go and restart your life somewhere far away." She offered a fake sincere smile. "Your dad is in good hands, if you're worried about leaving your old man behind." She chuckled like something was fucking funny.

"MAKE IT TWENTY-FIVE MILLION, sick ass bitch." My nostrils flared as I battled with keeping my cool.

"I WIPE my ass with that, I'll make it thirty. Good riddance Melvin." She dismissed me by looking away from me.

I WALKED OUT THE ROOM, satisfied with how my request went. I lost a lot from trying to please my father and sick ass Miguella. Right now, I had the perfect plan to get back on my shit. It took years for me to realize just how much I missed and loved Sovereign. I made a lot of mistakes along the way from having too much greed. I desperately wanted to find a way to get her fine ass back.

WHEN I FIRST GOT WITH Sovereign, I had a wife. I only got with Sovereign because Miguella wanted me to protect and keep a close eye on her granddaughter. At the time, my father was in debt and in too deep with Miguella for me to try to pull back. Miguella's reach was long back then and even now it still was.

MY FATHER and his men ran up in Sovereign's parent's house and shot her mother Sovereignty in the head right in front of Miguel. Miguel, Sovereign's father, had gone against the cartel and married Sovereignty. He was supposed to marry a woman back in Mexico that was picked out for him by Miguella. His punishment was Sovereignty's life and Sovereign as a later sacrifice.

That's just the surface of how conniving and selfish Miguella was. She used her family as a pawn all for her to maintain a certain amount of power in Mexico. She knew all about Queen running the streets and being raped while struggling to take care of her and Empress. She didn't give a damn what her granddaughters endured. I don't even think she loved them.

"YOU LEAVING?" I stopped and turned to face my father. I despised him most of the time but loved him all in the same breath.

"YEA, I'll be going to Vegas for a few months. I'll go check up on moms then contact you to make sure you're still breathing." He raised his thick bushy brows and walked towards me with his arms stretched open. I turned my back on him and shook my head. Opening the front door, I turned a little to see the disappointment on my father's face.

.   .   .

"I CAN'T BELIEVE you let an old bitch pimp you out like a hoe, pops. It's only a matter of time before she turns on you. Then here I come running, to get it back in blood for the sake of you." I slammed the door in his face. I wasn't going to Vegas, I just needed to throw them off of me. I pulled out my cellphone and pulled up my text thread.

I WAS HEADED to Callista's sexy ass house. I needed my nuts emptied in order to think clearer. I was considered the outcast, the bad guy. The nigga muthafuckas called themselves trying to hunt down. What was better than beating people at their own game when they went hunting for an enemy? Hiding in plain sight, when the time was right, I planned on popping up and taking what was mine. Sovereign.

LATER THAT NIGHT

I WATCHED my dick disappear down Callista's throat like she had some type of magic. She sucked my dick so good that I was moaning out like a bitch. Her throat suctioned tightly, each time she took me to the back of her throat. Pulling my dick out of her wet mouth, she tapped it on each side of her cheeks, then pushed it back down her throat.

"FUCKING, NASTY BITCH! SUCK DADDIES DICK!" I grabbed each side of her face and grunted, thrusting my hips, I started pushing in and out of her roughly. I was getting ready to explode. There was no greater feeling than releasing a good nut, next to getting money.

. . .

I FELT TONGUE TIDE, my nut shot down her tight throat and she swallowed all of my shit. Callista was my bitch for whenever I came to Mexico. She had an unlimited amount of money due to who her father was. I was put on to her through Miguella. Miguella was so grimy she worked with Callista and a couple others to be able to put a hit out on the Ruiz cartel.

THE HIT WASN'T to kill the head of the Ruiz cartel but to ruffle his feathers. Miguella wanted in on the golden triangle because it meant more power and resources. She also knew that he had an heir to the throne and planned on forcing Sovereign to marry Inferno in order to tie the two powerful families.

I laid back on the bed out of breath and feeling good. Callista hopped up to go in the bathroom to clean her face and brush her teeth. She was such a freak nasty bitch that she didn't care shit about catching her own nut. She got off on pleasing. I watched her saunter her sexy ass back in the room with a hot white towel.

SHE CLEANED my dick and giggled when it twitched in her hand from being sensitive.

"HOW LONG YOUR PARENTS GON' be gone for?" I pulled her up onto my chest, she closed her eyes and threw her leg over mine.

. . .

"A MONTH, they usually let me know when they're coming back. They like to vacation for long periods of time. Enjoying different countries." She smiled with her eyes closed. "Why, how long you staying?" She opened her eyes to stare at me.

"I'LL STAY until they return, I got to keep an eye on something. Plus, I can't get enough of this good ass head and wet ass pussy." I cupped her ass and squeezed tightly.

"OKAY, PAPI." She pecked my chest then got back comfortable on my chest. A couple of minutes later she was snoring softly on my chest as I thought of a master plan.

EMPRESS

$\mathcal{T}$his morning, I woke up in pain and panic. I was no longer being cared for by the unknown nurses and doctor that had checked in on me around the clock. Instead of seeing white walls, I woke up in a smaller room that had teal blue walls. The room smelled like eucalyptus and lavender. The walls were bare of any decorations or furniture. No TV nor medical equipment, I was laying on a hospital bed, with a hospital gown on. I moved the white sheets back and observed my side. Fresh bandaging covered the area where I was shot at.

I came to only one conclusion; Sovereign moved me and had me at an unknown location. I feared seeing or looking into my sister's eyes. I didn't want to see the hurt and disappointment plastered on her face. I knew in my heart that Queen would never forgive me for what I had done. She also would never trust me again.

I might've not acted like it or showed it but Sovereign was my lifeline. She was all I had, if I knew what I finally figured out now. I wish I could go back in time to the young me and make better decisions. Murk'um was dead because of me. I didn't know what hurt me more. His death or Sovereign never forgiving me.

I felt like shit, and I knew I looked even worse. The door-knob turning got my attention, my heart rate sped up, dread came over me and it felt like it took whoever was on the other side of that door forever to walk in.

I was unable to relax because I now feared the worst happening. My thoughts were racing and then everything seemed to go still as Sovereign walked into the room with an unreadable facial expression plastered on her face.

I gave her a sympathetic look, and that's when she let the unreadable facial expression go. Her eyes got glossy as she neared the bed. Sovereign smelled like heaven, as always, she was well-dressed. She walked and looked like money. She got to the side of my hospital bed and sat her YSL purse down. Opening it up, she pulled out a weave brush.

Her hair was neatly pulled back into a low ponytail, and her natural baby hair decorated her edges. I hadn't seen myself in days and I stopped counting the days after a week of being hooked up to different machines. I sighed hard as my tears started flowing. I didn't know what to say at first, so I whispered sorry to her. I couldn't even look her directly in the eyes because my guilty conscience was chewing away at my sanity.

"Don't speak, Empress just listen to me. I already know why you tried to rob Teddy." She peeked around my head and found the matted-down chunks of hair. Starting at the ends she softly brushed and detangled my hair. I closed my eyes and waited for Sovereign to say something.

The silence and the sound of her breathing was eating away at me. Her first set of words broke the damn and my tears started flowing at a rapid pace.

"You really hurt me, Empress. It makes me wonder what

all you have been hiding from me." She paused and my stomach tightened. The best thing for me to do right now was to remain quiet and not say a thing.

I didn't know how she even knew, how or why I tried to rob Teddy. That in itself had me paranoid. If she knew about me and Melvin, then she probably wouldn't be brushing my hair.

"My husband keeps trying to convince me that the people I love are trying to betray and hurt me for the worse. I feel like it's bullshit, but then again after I discovered that our father was still alive and hiding from us…" she paused and this time I turned to look at her. Maybe it was the medication that had me hearing shit. Did she just say our father was alive?

"Yea, you heard me correctly. Our father is alive, I discovered that shit three weeks ago when I went on a mission to kill a husband and wife that our Abuela put a hit out on. She didn't give me a reason for the hit. Abuela just said that they were enemies and it had to be done, in order for her to help me find Melvin." She stopped talking and moved to the other side of my hospital bed, to start on the other side of my hair.

The mention of Melvin's name had me sweating and I hoped that she couldn't see the change in my demeanor from just mentioning that man's name.

"When I get there, I'm ready to kill until an old ass man calls me by my government name. He claimed he leaves his front and back door open for me. He knew that one day, I would come. I find out he's our uncle and dad came down the hallway to see whom his uncle was talking to." She started brushing through my hair a little rough and nervousness took back over me as she started to giggle softly.

To a person that didn't know Sovereign, they would relax

thinking shit was cool because she was giggling like something was hilarious to her. This was my big sister, and I knew her better than I knew myself. Sovereign was angry as fuck. "Can you believe that I fainted? I became so overwhelmed with emotions!" She yelled and her voice bounced off the walls. She stopped brushing my hair as she stepped away from the bed and placed her hands on her hips. She started to pace back in forth with her fist clenching tight.

"I was emotional and angry, hurt and some more shit! My father was still alive after all the fucked up shit I had to go through to provide for your ungrateful entitled ass! I did shit that I would never forgive myself for! All for you to rob Teddy because you didn't like that I gave him a position that he didn't ask for!" She was no longer looking at me, she was about to go into one of her maniac episodes. It was best for me to just listen and pray that she didn't hurt me.

"I mean this nigga alive and doing just fine!" she spat bitterly, a tear escaped her eye and my heart broke. "I had to marry a stranger, who happens to almost be a little crazier than me. I haven't known the nigga that long but a sick part of me likes him. I'm a fuckin Queenpin, I'm rich as fuck but I'm only in the position that I am in now because of our backstabbing grandmother who had our mother executed and our father outcasted."

Sovereign placed her hands on her knees and howled like a coyote. I couldn't decipher if she was laughing too hard or sobbing. She caught her breath and gave me an icy glare.

"I watched our father take my gun and shoot our uncle in the head. He didn't want Abuela to know that I didn't complete the mission that she sent me on. Then he went to the back of the house and killed our aunt, while she was sleeping. I took pictures and sent them over to Abuela from our uncle's phone so she could know the mission was complete."

Sovereign was hysterical, the wild look in her eyes showed that she was having a hard time processing everything.

"Why the fuck did I go along with what Papa told me to do after I felt like he betrayed us too? I don't fucking know! He gave me his number and disappeared out the back door. After the mission was complete, I paid a visit to Abuela." I watched my sister take a seat on the tile floor and fold her legs until she was sitting Indian style. She rocked back and forth, her eyes connected with mine, I wished I could get up and hold her.

"That old ass vindictive bitch, smiled in my face and poured us up glasses of the finest champagne in Mexico and toasted to new money and power." She pointed at her purse, and I reached to the side of me and grabbed it. Making sure it was closed, I tossed it her way. She opened it up and pulled out a blunt along with a lighter.

After sparking her blunt, she inhaled deeply then exhaled.

"I disappeared for a while; I can't trust none of y'all. So, I disappeared to sort my thoughts. While I was away…. I realized that my heart became colder, that shit is frozen." She pulled her gun out of her purse and stood up from the floor. I stopped breathing momentarily to gauge what was going on.

"I can look deep into those troubled eyes, Empress…. There's more to you but I wouldn't know because you a flaw ass bitch. Selfish and dirty like our Abuela and father."

I shivered as she caressed my cheek with the tip of her gun.

"I want to kill you Empress, I can't because I love you. I raised you… I thought I did a good job at doing that but it's obvious that it's something I failed at."

My bottom lip started to tremble, and I could no longer

hold back or hide the fear that was lodged inside of me. Sovereign had a wild look in her eyes. The bags that sat underneath her eyes were heavy like she did a lot of crying and worrying.

"I never meant to hurt you, Sovereign." My voice cracked.

"You did hurt me." She snickered and then wiped her nose. "I ain't no weak ass bitch, hurt becomes numb after so long you know?" She turned her gun to the butt and cocked it back like she was about to crush my face in. Something was holding her back as I clenched the sheet tightly in my shaking hands.

"Fuck!!!!" I jumped at her elevated tone of voice. Her shoulders dropped first, followed by her bowing her head. She turned away from me and it felt like I could breathe again.

I watched her walk to retrieve her expensive purse. She placed the gun back inside and then turned to walk towards the door.

"Papa is waiting for you, outside of this door. Since he's in hiding, I guess you should go hide with him. Don't let me ever see your face again Empress. Don't reach out to me. I'm cutting ties with you. I'm gonna prove to you, Papa, and Abuela that I'm far from a weak ass bitch. You have twenty-four hours to get your ass far away from me." Her hand touched the door as I called her name to stop her.

I thought of all the things that I had done behind her back. I wanted to confess but I knew if I did that it would force her to take that gun back out and blow my head off. I almost had the courage, but staring at my conflicted sister, I dropped my eyes and simpered lowly.

"I love you, and I'm sorry." It felt like someone was dragging a knife down the middle of my heart.

15

"I love you too, Empress, love ain't enough. I tried to give you this time to admit to all the shit you have done. Even with my ex Melvin the nigga you knew that I once loved, yet you still opened up your legs and fucked him. You helped him kidnap Princess and mourned the lost with me. I love you but I hate you just as much bitch. You ain't shit but a low barrel dirty ass bitch. One day you gon' hate yourself more then I even hate you. I cried so much silently over the years behind yo dog ass. Your betrayal I put to the back of my mind because you're my blood sister. You know me better than anybody walking this earth, so I don't see how you thought you was getting away with some shit bitch. This was your opportunity to revive yourself, but you failed with that. Fuck you..." She walked out, closing the door softly. I wailed like a baby until I felt dizzy. I deserved everything that was happening. I thought of Murk'um and cried even harder.

I thought back to all the times my sister gave me dirty looks and it was because she knew all this time. She was waiting for me to admit my wrongs. She was willing to forgive me, and I just ruined that.

"Princessa." My Papa and I locked eyes. His face mirrored mine, I started to sob even harder. Happy to see him alive and standing. His salt and pepper goatee were neatly trimmed, his hair was short and curly with flecks of white hair scattered throughout his head.

"What all have you done?" He grabbed the folding chair that sat in far-right corner of the room and pulled it close to the side of my hospital bed. Grabbing my hand brought comfort to me, that I didn't know I needed. I took a deep breath and let the reality of my dad being well and alive hit me first. I started from the beginning telling him all the things Sovereign and I endured and what led up to me sleeping with Melvin, behind Sovereign's back.

We cried and held hands tight when I went into deeper detail of Sovereign. A lot of times my sister thought I wasn't aware or didn't see the bruises and her lying in bed crying at night. Some nights she would fall asleep in the bathtub, crying herself to sleep. I remember the sound of her young voice sounding frantic as she would mumble things to herself while soaking.

Back then, Sovereign treated me like a delicate flower. She made sure she watered me, no matter the dark thick cloud that followed her around. Sovereign wanted me to bloom into something great and I miserably failed at that. Deep down, Sovereign knew that keeping me alive would be torturous enough. I had to live my life far away from her and that would be a hard task. I would be left to think about my actions and fucked up ways with no chance of her forgiving me.

"You messed up, Princessa. Not as bad as me, I became so depressed and overwhelmed by the murder of your mother." He stopped talking as I watched him swallow down hard. "I have no excuse, Princessa. Your mother was my soul mate, I should have let her live her life and raise you guys with me in Mexico. I should have held up to my end of the deal with you guys Abuela. I just loved Sovereignty too much to marry a strange woman that I didn't see myself being with. I thought my mother would understand this, I never expected her to send Melvin Sr. to assassinate your mother." He didn't bother wiping the tear that fell down his round face.

"Sovereign sacrificed for Abuela, and now I feel as if she is in danger. She married into the cartel, there is no backing out. Where does Abuela think you're at?" I really wanted to know because now my head was starting to spin. I betrayed my sister for a man that really did have something to do with

17

my mother's death. It didn't have to be Melvin that pulled the trigger on my mother. His father was close enough.

I should have never helped Melvin escape; he would've been better off dead at the hands of Sovereign.

"Miguella, thinks I'm in Cuba. After she put the hit out on Sovereignty, she forced me to stay away from you two and to never be seen again. She had no clue of me sneaking in and out of Mexico, staying with your uncle. I only kept sneaking back and forth in hopes to run into Sovereign. It's so much to it Princessa, I will tell you more, but we have to leave now while we both are under the radar. We will figure everything out in due time. Right now, we really have to go." He looked at me with pleading eyes.

Growing up, I never saw the fear that I was seeing now from my father. It disgusted me, because no matter how mad Sovereign was with me, I didn't want to leave her to figure all of this out. She was a pawn to my Abuela, and I wouldn't be able to live if something happened to her.

"Princessa, I know, I have been a coward. Leaving the two of you as young girls. Just trust me, even if it's momentarily. When the time is right, I will kill Miguella and make sure my daughter is okay. Right now, Sovereign is not going to bend when it comes to forgiveness. We have to play the background."

My father was right about that. Sovereign was in a different mental space. I saw it in her eyes, the confliction and the pain. I said a silent prayer as my father helped me stand. I just prayed that God could let Sovereign see that I was very sorry and was ready to now do right by her. My gut was telling me though, that it was too late. I knew already that things would never be the same.

QUEEN

I was a very self-assured person, nothing at this stage of my life could take a jab at my self-esteem. I went through a very low stage in my life, when I felt low, ugly, and unworthy. After sleeping with more men than I could count unwillingly before I even hit my twenties. I became a strong young girl with a vision to make it out of just feeling low and struggling.

I remember chanting to myself while looking in the mirror at the age of sixteen. Telling myself that I was beautiful, and I would one day have the world eating out the palm of my hands. By the time I was eighteen, I became fully self-assured, I didn't need a man telling me how beautiful I was just to get between my smooth thick thighs. After sacrificing my body so much throughout my teens. I made sure when I no longer had to revert back to having sex for money that it was for my pleasure.

Before I knew it, experiencing climaxes was like therapy. It momentarily took me to another dimension and eased my rattled nerves.

I wasn't the best at everything I did, but I tried to be. In my eyes, even the strongest powerful man had a weak point, in most men that weak point was pussy.

With Inferno, I couldn't quite figure that weak point out. I know I vowed to never get caught so caught up into a man to the point that I feel hooked and trapped. Yet here I sat in the dark, inhaling the woodsy burnt smell that permeated the space in his room. Hades, is what he loved to call this wing of his home. Right now, I was so sure of myself. Yet so conflicted about being here asking for something that would relieve my problems momentarily. With a heavy heart and feeling vulnerable, I knew that only Malice could take care of that so I could think clearly, even if it was for just an hour.

I tried calling the twins before I even thought about coming here. The twin's number was disconnected which had me pissed off. Malice scared them shitless and that lowkey pissed me off because Aiden and Caiden were actually my friends and I enjoyed spending time with them to get my mind off of my actual reality. With the twins, I didn't have to act hardcore. I could just chill and vibe, they made me laugh and feel good beyond the sex.

I couldn't get Empress or my father off my mind for the life of me. I had business to tend to and I was starting to feel like that unsure weak young, minded girl from the past. I needed to reboot and get my shit together. Sex, good sex is what I needed.

For the past couple of weeks, I've been chanting and trying to force the two people that I truly loved to the back of my mental. I still had to put up a facade when it came to my Abuela. That was going to be a hard task.

There was one thing I didn't do, and that was lie and a fraud. With my Abuela, I still had to go about things as if I wasn't on to her until the timing was right. I wanted to put Melvin in the dirt and really take over her cartel as well as putting my gang on. Now that I knew what role she played, me wanting the cartel was a faraway thought. I no longer wanted parts in anything this bitch created. I wanted blood, her blood since she had my mother killed.

My heart rate increased, and excitement flowed throughout my entire being when the door to Malice room door opened. Hearing him clap his hands for the lights to come on had me anxious to see his shocked expression when he realized I intruded into his personal space. Disappointment became evident on my face as I watched his housemaid look at me with wide eyes as she watched me sit at the edge of his bed in the dark with a lit blunt.

"I'm so sorry, Malice is on the south wing and wanted me to have his things ready for when he returned to Hades." I nodded my head and offered her a small smile. She was a beautiful older Hispanic lady; her hair was neatly pulled back into a perfect tight bun. She wore red scrubs; in her hand she held a salad along with a glass of Cognac. What an odd mix. She sat the salad and drink down and walked up to his dresser, pulling out a pair of silk pajamas.

"What's your name?" She looked up at me and smiled. Her smile was a genuine smile like she loved what she did for work. That was a little surprising, I imagined Malice being an asshole to the people that worked for him. With her that didn't seem to be the case.

"My name is Julia. I am the head-house maid. If you ever have any problems with my staff, please let me know." She bowed a little and smiled at me. Her smile was contagious, so I offered her one back.

"Sure thing, nice to meet you, Julia. I'm Sovereign, if you mind me asking when will Malice retreat back to Hades?" I was probably reaching at this point; I hope my desperation to get fucked wasn't too obvious. I didn't give a damn though,

Malice had to be good for something. If making me cum until my stomach cramped up was one of them then so be it.

"He usually works late at this hour. Kenya Monroe is very thorough at what she does at the end of each month." She clamped her lips tight like she said too much the fear was evident on her facial expression. I gave her a reassuring smile and winked at her. It was a silent form of me communicating to her that I wouldn't tell her boss on her.

"Would you like me to get you some of my special herbal tea?" She quickly changed the subject. I watched her grab onto her pants and then release it. She definitely was now nervous.

"No, Julia. The last time I drank your tea… I woke up in Mexico on a private jet. I might get some later, sleep has been hard to come by lately." I surprised myself at exposing that. I hadn't had a full night sleep since everything went down with my Papa.

"I want you to lead the way to my husband, and Ms. Kenya Monroe." I stood up from the bed and walked to Malice side. Picking up his glass of Cognac, I took it back with a couple of gulps then cracked my neck side to side. I needed a good ass body massage and some good ass weed to release all this tension I had bottled in.

"Do you have some more of this? This is the smoothest cognac that I have ever tasted. What brand?" I was intrigued by how smooth it went down my throat.

"That is my Excellency's favorite." She smiled proudly; I rolled my eyes at what she referred to him as. "Henri IV Dudognon Heritage Cognac, Grande Champagne. Very dangerous drink. It's known as the DNA of Cognac." She talked highly of the drink that danced around on my taste buds. I suddenly wanted more as I could feel the small effects of it.

"How much does it go for?" I tilted the glass to see if it was at least a drop left.

"Two million dollars." I shook my head at the ridiculous price but kept the glass in my hand.

"Take me to him, I want another full cup." I added, walking past her to the door.

"You sure? One glass does the trick." She looked at me with worry.

"A person like me might need the entire bottle." I opened the room door and was met by an expensive mini-Golf cart. I giggled a little feeling the effects of just that one cup of cognac. This man had his staff riding around in his mansion on golf carts. I never saw such a thing. She came out the door behind me and went to the back of the golf cart, lifting the trunk up. Pulling out a chilled expensive crystal bottle that looked like it was covered with expensive gold, the top looked like it had real diamonds scattered all over it. For two million dollars the gold and the diamonds had to be real.

I wondered how long this niggas money was to have this drink for his nightcap. She walked cautiously with the bottle and carefully removed the top. Julia handled the glass bottle like her life was on the line as she poured me a full glass. I took slow sips as I eased into the seat and waited for her to put the bottle back into the trunk of the golf cart. I thanked Julia once she got situated behind the wheel and took in Malice's mansion.

I never took this place in, since the first time I was here, I was brought against my will. The second time, I broke in through the back. Now that I was looking, this place had to of cost him a fortune.

Malice's mansion exuded every essence of luxury, elegance, and comfort. It sat on a small acreage with a relaxing view of the city. As we rode through the huge house,

I couldn't deny that it was impeccable. This place was made of concrete and tall glass windows. We passed the front of the mansion, and I became lost in the beauty of it.

This shit was past fancy as hell. Gold fixtures and statues decorated the huge space, making it stand out and capture your attention. The white couches were tufted with gold and beige pillows sitting up perfectly on each end. I fell in love with the big glass chandeliers that sat right in front of the arched glass window. I imagined how beautiful the chandeliers crystals looked when the sun shined in the front of the house.

We went down a long and wide hallway that had a floating chandelier and recessed lighting that looked magical as hell. We had been riding in this golf cart for about three minutes, until she finally came to a stop in front of two big double doors. Each side of the double door had fire flames engraved.

"This is, Excellency library office. He should be in here." She offered me a nervous smile as I nodded my head. I took another sip of the smooth expensive cognac and stepped out of the cart. I was dressed down in black Nike leggings with a black and white crop top Nike shirt. On my feet were some comfortable Nike sandals. I hadn't done much to my curly hair today, it was wild and all over my head. Tucking some hair behind my ears, I watched Julia knock on the door and take a couple of steps back.

A couple of seconds later the door opened on its own. I couldn't even focus on Malice because this was another huge ass space. From the floor to ceiling, books aligned the walls. I couldn't even see what color the wall was because the thousands of books served as the wall with hundreds of shelves. So, he was a book worm too. I chuckled at that and stepped into the room. Malice looked up from his desk and stared hard at me, without saying shit. He had a laptop opened with his phone in his hand. The need to have my pussy roughly stroked by him had my clit jumping. I licked my lips as Julia walked up to his desk and spoke in a hushed tone. Malice remained quiet and nodded his head once. He thanked her and then turned his attention back to me. His expressive stare had me speechless and he knew the shit. He smirked cockily at me and stood up.

"Breaking into my house?" His eyes landed on the glass cup that was supposed to be meant for him. Those two-toned perfect eyes of his looked back into my orbs. I could've sworn his beautiful eyes darkened as he continued to stare.

"Breaking into my home and drinking my special drink." He added as he stepped around his desk. I heard the sound of someone clearing their throat, I broke eye contact with Malice. My eyes landed on Kenya. I couldn't lie or hate and say that she was ugly. That was not the case with Kenya. She was beautiful as hell and had a banging ass body.

When I looked into her eyes, I saw jealousy. I smiled at her and took in the small space she was working in compared to the area Malice had for himself. You could tell they were really working on something concerning his syndicate. The silk spaghetti strapped dress she had on with a high split that gave me a view of her red lace panties, gave off the indication that she was expecting something from Malice after work.

Her hair was pulled up into a neat slick high bun, with diamond earrings that drooped down a little from the weight.

"I came in here to tell you that your snack is in Hades, awaiting you now. Go ahead and page Julia so she can make two trips from picking us up." I looked right into his eyes waiting for him to play dumb with me.

"I'd prefer if you left first. I will make sure your guest wrap up whatever the fuck she was doing dear?" I almost laughed but kept my face blank. Malice gave me an amused look. He picked up his walkie talkie and spoke in Spanish to Julia. When he was done, he placed it back down on his desk and came to stand in front of me.

His smell was so manly and sexy, I felt myself swooning. My clit thumped hard, as excitement flowed throughout me. I couldn't wait for Malice to get deep inside of me and relieve me, so I could feel somewhat in touch.

"I'll call you tomorrow, Kenya." Was all he said to her, he never looked her way as he touched the side of my face with his warm rough hand. His fingertips tickled my high cheekbone as he went to lean in closer. I froze up a bit because I wasn't the kissing type of female. Malice knew this already. I guess since I came in here demanding shit in front of this bitch. Malice planned on having some fun with this entire situation.

He leaned down with his tall frame hovering over mine. Looking deep into my eyes, it got too intense, so I focused on the burn mark along his jawline. The burn mark started from his ear and ended two inches away from his chin. Before I could place my eyes back onto him, he stole my breath away by kissing me deeply, while holding my chin tight with the tip of his burnt rough fingertips.

He kissed me so deeply that he forced me to moan into his mouth. I held onto his broad muscular shoulders. When he released me, he walked past me and slapped me hard on the ass, snapping me right out of my trance. I was stuck in place for a couple of seconds too long before I gave Kenya my attention.

Her eyes were blazing right into mine. I couldn't hold my laugh in any longer, so when the door closed, I doubled over and laughed hard as fuck. When I looked over at her, I moved close to her with glossy eyes. Kenya looked at me like I had shit on my face. I kept the same silly grin on my face.

Sitting at the edge of her small ass desk, I shook my head then shrugged my shoulders.

"Niggas like that, only become head over hills for a bitch that's hard to obtain." I schooled her, looking down at my nail bed.

"Like you?" I eyed her and nodded my head yes.

"Definitely like me, Kenya. You have nothing to worry about though, I don't want him the way that you do. I just want to experience him sexually. I think we can both agree that sexually, the man is beyond blessed." I giggled and kicked my feet back and forth.

"This marriage and what we have is business, I'm sure he has told you that. Beyond that though, Kenya. I come first to him, before any other bitch that got a wet pussy between their legs. He's so caught up in me, because I'm not some bitch running around this muthafucka with my head cut off." I let my words marinate for a while, as bad as she was trying to play things off smooth, the redness in her cheeks said otherwise.

"When the time is right... I'll turn him loose, maybe."

"Maybe?" She raised her brows.

"Yes, bitch maybe. I don't know Kenya. I'm starting to think me, and my husband are a lot alike. So, if I find myself not wanting to turn him loose, only then you should be worried, because if I consider him a hundred percent mine... then there is a strong chance that you could possibly lose your life. You're such a pretty ass woman, who can find another handsome man to play around with. Take my advice Kenya and grow some balls like the imaginary big ones I got. Inferno knows my balls are bigger and hang lower than his." I winked at her and stood up.

Walking towards the door, I stopped and looked over my shoulder.

"Let Julia or whoever that's in charge, to lock up behind you. When I am here, I'm the woman of the house. There will be no spending the night like we sister wives and shit." I chuckled and was happy to see Julia waiting for me outside the electric double doors.

Once I got seated, I tossed the rest of the smooth cognac down. I rotated my neck and wished that I could pre-stretch my body. Malice was about to give me that work, I could feel it from the kiss alone.

MALICE

The air stilled. My room seemed to fall silent as well. Sovereign entered and had me captivated by her beauty. I never knew what it felt like to miss a woman, until Sovereign showed her face. She made me forget that Kenya and I was working on something important. Her sweet sexy smell filled my room. Sovereign reeked of confidence, a confidence that was hard to come by in people.

My confidence matched hers, and I think that's what made her a million times more appealing. I could look into her eyes and see the raw battle that she was up against. She remained strong and solid but the small bags under those hazel eyes of hers showed some form of struggle. Something happened the night of her going to kill for Miguella. I needed to know what that something was. I was going to get to the bottom of it. It didn't matter that I didn't like our arrangement of being married. She was now a Ruiz and I wanted to protect and solve her problems as if they were mine.

"Strip and come here." I sat at the edge of the bed. Sovereign had an air of danger attached to her that I welcomed like the burning fires in my chamber. I was drawn to her like a moth to a bright flame. I wanted to unravel her and figure her deepest mysteries out. Fuck I'm talking crazy, but I can't even help myself. As soon as my lips touched hers back in my library, my body felt like it was on fire. I wanted to take her ass all the way down right in front of Kenya. My dick was hard, and it started to ache with anticipation. Sovereign came here for something, that something was in her lustful stare as she peeled off every piece of clothing.

"You miss me?" I didn't answer, if I did, I was putting myself at her mercy. I wasn't going to allow her to break me down like I was ready to do to her. She stepped out of her panties, and I took her in slowly from head to toe. Starting at her teal blue chunky toes I stopped at her thick ankles that were strong when she locked her feet behind my back. My eyes traveled to her legs which looked shiny and smooth, and I stopped my eyes from roaming and looked at her kneecaps. They weren't dark, they were the same color as the rest of her skin. Had she ever fallen on her knees like I did when she was a kid? Did she ever drop down to those knees and give a nigga head? I felt like she was that perfect, I wouldn't be surprised if she didn't even give head. Her thick fucking thighs kept that fat pussy warm. I counted at least seven to six dimples in each thigh.

Then her stomach, she had enough to hold onto and caress, I enjoyed how fluffy her stomach felt up against my hard abs as I pounded inside of her. When I got to her breast, I licked my lips. She broke my thoughts as she spoke and stepped closer to me, until she was standing between my legs.

"It's evident that you miss me." She placed her cold hands on my shoulders. Instinctively my hands found her round soft ass. I didn't know if I wanted to squeeze it, slap it or just simply grab the deep cuff that should've put a lot of pressure on her back. Sovereign had so much ass on her, it was surprising how she strutted so hard toting some heavy shit like she had behind her.

I pulled her close and buried my nose into her navel, inhaling her scent deeply. Then releasing as I looked up into her eyes.

"You have been running from me." She pushed me back and if I had used a little of my strength I probably wouldn't have bulged. Seeing the hunger in her eyes, I laid back and allowed her to climb right on top of me, like the tallest tree out in the middle of the woods.

Locking my hands behind my head, I watched her and every move she made. I laid there with excitement; I was still fully clothed. Sovereign started at my Alexander McQueen button-up shirt. She ripped it open while biting her bottom lip. She ignored the buttons popping everywhere and went right to my all-black slacks.

Once she undid my belt and unzipped my pants, she got into a squatting position and slowly lowered her blazing tunnel onto my dick. I made it jump to throw her off a little. She giggled but then looked at me seriously like she was getting ready to claim and take my dick as hers.

I slid my hands around her waist and pushed her all the way down my long thick length. She hissed and resituated herself. Her toes curled tightly, she placed her hands on my chest and bounced up and down at her own tempo. My hands slowly fell away from her waist as I tried to steady my own damn breathing.

Her pouty lips parted like she wanted to say something, but she was too full of dick. Sovereign grabbed her succulent full breast and squeezed them tightly. I looked at how wide her legs were opened and how the inside of her thighs glistened and felt the blood rush straight to the head of my dick.

Sovereign was wet as fuck, so wet that the sound of her pussy was starting to become my favorite sound as it bounced off my dark walls. Waves of her sweet smell kept hitting me, her eyes kept shutting and opening like she was concentrating on riding out the strong wave to her first orgasm. My hand grazed the bottom of her stomach and went right between those sexy thick thighs. I slid my fingers between her wet folds until I found her clit. Popping it first then strumming that swollen bud slowly, I coached her into her first orgasm of the night.

"Cum for me first baby, I'll arrive later," I reassured her. I didn't care that Sovereign didn't make much noise during this session. Her body language was talking loud and clear, each time her tight ass pussy contracted on my dick was another indication that she was getting exactly what the fuck she wanted.

Her body was trembling and shaking, like I was snatching her soul away.

"Shit!" She hissed out, a moan slipped from her lips. I wanted to take over and be in control. I was trying to let her catch her first nut because the next round was all on me and taking over her entire fucking body. I wanted to be lodged in Sovereigns wet dreams, good dreams and even nightmares.

I couldn't deny the connection between us, even if I wanted to. Sovereign was crazy in the fucking head if she thought I would be letting up on her anytime soon. This marriage was starting to feel real, like it was meant for this arrangement to be.

"Maliceee." My name rolled sexily off her tongue. Her head fell back exposing the small stretch marks between her armpits, leading to the fatty part of her arm.

"Say that shit, Sovereign," I grunted feeling myself about to release deep inside of her. Sovereign sped up her pace, her pussy felt like it was vacuuming the nut right out of my dick. Her shit squeezed me so tight that it hurt because it felt so fucking good.

I drew blood, biting down on my bottom lip, watching her tremble and shake hard right on top of me, had to be the sexiest shit ever.

"Maliceeee!!!!" She said my name like she was asking a question. Did she want my permission to release all of what she had right on my dick? I slapped both ass cheeks and gripped them tight. Separating her cheeks apart, I pushed upward roughly inside her snug tunnel.

"Let that shit the fuck go," I grunted and demanded, watching her unravel was a beautiful sight. Collapsing right on top of me, breathing hard as fuck. I glided my hand up her back which was drenched with sweat.

"My turn now, Sovereign." She mumbled something that I didn't understand. I let her catch her breath because I already knew what I was getting ready to do to her.

Before I got my turn, Sovereign was snoring softly. I shook my head and let her remain just how she was. She looked like she was at peace and for some reason, I felt like she needed it. Her curly hair was wild and damp, a couple of loose strands stuck to her pretty round face. I never watched a woman as hard as I was watching Sovereign.

Some men got turned on by a woman that was super soft and dainty. A woman that was submissive and trusted a man without him having to prove why he should be trusted. A woman that wanted to be left in the dark about all the fucked up and dark things her man did. They never wanted to see the monster side of their man, only the good things. Not Sovereign, she was crafted and created more differently.

Her hands got just as dirty as mine, she led a pack of hungry wolves and they followed. Her men trusted that her decisions would be the right ones so it could ensure the next meal their families ate. She was a getting money beast, smart as fuck and the biggest trait that turned me on the most about her was the loyalty that I saw deep inside her hazel brown eyes.

Sovereign had been betrayed more times than she knew about. Hurt by the closest people, she kept inside of her heart. I watched her for countless minutes until she stirred and her sleep and moved off of me and onto her side. Her eyes opened slowly as I looked up to see the time on the wall. We had been lying like this for hours, it was now three in the morning.

"I slept with men for money." She whispered lowly. She sighed as she looked up into my eyes, I remained quiet because I knew it was more coming.

"When my parents disappeared out of me and Empress life, I stepped up for my sister and I. At first, we had hand-outs, folks letting us live with them and some nights we slept where we could. Until my friend, well ex-friend, Saleema, she introduced us to her big brother Salem. They were both a big blessing. Took us in, clothed and fed us. Not even after a full month, I had to sacrifice instead of running away. I got broken in. He was my first, at thirteen and then after him, there were so many other men for a small or big fee that I stopped counting." She sat up with her back facing me. Pulling her knees up to her chest, she continued as my anger rose high. I already started making plans on hunting down this nigga and burning him alive.

"I was weak and broken at that age. I used to feel like since I was fat my body was what men wanted because they mistakenly thought that I had breast, hips and ass when at the time it was just baby fat traveling to those areas to make me appear more grown. I'd rather it be me than my sister." She stood up and looked around the room until her eyes landed on my ashtray. Julia always rolled me up a couple of blunts, so that when I retreated to my room. I could relax in peace. "I got pregnant by Salem and was taken to a hood doctor, that fucked my insides up. I still feel haunted by that abortion, and I count each year and mentally celebrate my unborn child's birthday. To punish myself, I forget all about my own birthday and don't celebrate it." I could hear my torch lighting up the blunt that was now between her lips. She sparked it and the smoke decorated the air.

"After being fucked and treated like shit, I found my backbone years later and roamed the streets more. I used my body as a weapon until I formed a masterpiece in the streets. I created my own family and met another man. His name was Melvin. Cut a long story short, I fell in love with Melvin. I loved how he made me feel protected. He made me feel like every woman should feel. I became even stronger, and I start seeing myself as beautiful. Melvin respected me as a Queen, his queen. Until another man that still loves me and wants to be with me revealed to me more then what I could handle. Pictures, was given to me of Melvin with a pregnant wife." She turned around to face me and her face was void of emotion. Her voice was flat, like what she was saying didn't bother her much.

"That's not even what hurt me the most." She paused and looked up at the ceiling, releasing the smoke that she held inside of her. When her eyes focused back on me, she chuckled and sniveled as slow tears dampened her face.

"The next couple of pictures were photos of him and my sister Empress. I stood in front of Bundy wondering if I should kill him, but I let him hold me and kiss all over me. We connected at that moment, but I stepped away from him to figure out what it was I wanted to do. Bundy saw me while

I was weak, and I hated that. He saw me become conflicted with doing what a Queenpin should have done at the time. Rather she was my blood or not I should have killed Empress, but I couldn't because I fucking love her and she's my blood sister. I raised her and helped make sure that she was straight. I thought to myself like damn, Sovereign! What good example had I set for her? All she ever seen me do was lay up and get dicked down to provide. She probably would hear me crying at night almost drowning myself in the tub with my sorrows. I wasn't there emotionally for her, so she found that in a man that preyed on her being young and vulnerable. I thought that maybe one day when she matured, she'd see her wrongdoing and confess but she never did. I let it go and me and Bundy created an unspoken agreement."

She wiped her face hard, and I sat up and moved to the edge of the bed to stand and go console her, but she shook her head no. I remained seated and watched her battle with her emotions.

"I tucked that shit and still took care of Empress. Out of loyalty and our bloodline. I made countless excuses for her when I found myself buried in my thoughts about her loyalty. Throughout the years, I wondered if it was her that helped Melvin escape. I still don't know but looking into her eyes while I expressed my disappointment in her, I saw the confirmation. I thought making her and Murk'um bring that nigga to me and watch all the evil things I had done to him and his wife that it will be a lesson to her as well. Obviously, it wasn't because she turned around and did some more fuck shit with Teddy."

"She sat up and tried to rob a boy that she knows I care for. Teddy wasn't dealt a good hand and he doesn't ask for handouts when it comes to shit. I keep spinning that shit, what if her fucked up plan really worked? Teddy wouldn't be here and who would his sisters have? Empress is such a selfish bitch, but I now understand who she gets that shit from." She took a deep pull from her blunt and gave me a look that had her eyes darkening.

"Our father, Miguel. That's who she gets it from." She shook her head and blew smoke out of her mouth. "He's still alive after all this time. I'm thinking he's dead, I done went through all of this shit and degrading because I thought both parents were dead. All of it for nothing."

"It was for something; it was in the cards that you were dealt. If you hadn't been dealt those cards you wouldn't have become the strong ass woman you are today Sovereign. You wouldn't be a Queenpin and be able to say that you created that shit on your own." I stood up and made my way over to her. Sovereign smelled so good even though she just got through sweating and fucking me hard. I had to focus because I was ready to pick her up and fuck every issue and problem that fucked with her.

In my eyes, she ain't have to worry about none of that shit. I had come into her life, and even though it was from an arranged marriage to create power. I planned on making her life easier.

"You keep thinking about the past and letting that shit define you, you will be stuck in that shit. Look at my father, nigga got enough money for me and all of his kids plus his great grands to never work or lift a finger. Deep down he ain't happy, all he got is his cartel. He got to sit from the sidelines and watch the woman of his dreams and the woman he truly loves, search high and low to replace him. He still stuck thinking about the past and what all could've been done differently." That opened my eyes to why I never settled on love. I never wanted to be like my dad or my mom.

I didn't want to experience loving someone all for them to

betray or do me foul. I also didn't want to have a good ass woman that I did truly love like my dad with my mom and then lose her because I couldn't get my shit right.

"We can play the blame game all night Sovereign. I ain't saying this shit to make you think that I'm just some heartless ass nigga. I'm saying this shit because you can't hold shit against people for who they truly are. You can't try to think because you love a muthafucka they supposed to love you the same and do you the same as you do them. People expose who the fuck they are, and you have to treat them accordingly. I'm not you though and you are not me and I understand that you feel how you feel. Disappearing and trying to sort this shit out alone ain't healthy." I pulled her close, but she stepped out of my embrace.

"All I have is me now, I vowed to myself that I would kill the head of my problems." She had a determined look in her eyes that I couldn't knock her for.

"What we have is an arrangement, but you have been giving me lethal ass dick. I'm telling you all of this because I don't want you falling for me Malice. I'm fucked up and you got the kind of dick that goes along with your persona perfectly. The type of shit you packing will have a bitch hooked and if are when I become hooked on you, I will annihilate any person that I feel will cause a fucking problem. Your handsome and you turn me on every time your crazy ass comes near me. I like your infatuation with fire on some straight nutty shit. I came here tonight to use you as a release, like a drug to get high off of. I realized that I'm close to getting hooked but the red flags about you is evident. That's the only reason why I'm exposing so much." She tilted her head back a little to look me in the eyes.

In this moment everything she said had me stuck and

speechless. I came back down to reality when her soft fingertips caressed my abs.

"You are my husband and it's unethical what we have
done to step into more power, but I like the shit. I know it's
going to probably come to an ugly end once I get what I need
out of my Abuela and that's Melvin. After that, I will be
killing her and getting redemption on everyone involved in
killing my mother. I have no plans stepping into her shoes
and running her fucked up cartel. Then my need for you will
go away. Your father will no longer see me as a good candi-
date and he would want to do away with me, then there's a
war between me and your cartel as well as your syndicate.
None of that scares me Malice because if I have to go to war I
will until one of us comes out on top." She smiled and tried to
walk away but I grabbed her by the arm and pulled her back
into me.

I said nothing as I kissed her deeply. At first, she didn't
kiss me back but after a couple of seconds she gave into the
kiss. I grabbed a handful of hair and yanked it until her neck
was exposed to me.

"It wouldn't be a war, Sovereign. You are my wife, and
you signed those terms of service. You're confused now with
your feelings and that's cool because I am too. We can take
this shit slow but I ain't letting up on you. Your mine. All
mine, all the other shit we can figure out. You're a Ruiz now
and that's not changing. So, if you want Miguella's cartel to
die out then it will. I have no plans on taking over my father's
cartel." I spoke truthfully to her and then led her to my walk-
in closet. I didn't want to run his cartel; I had my own shit
that was thriving bigger than a bunch of old ass rules that my
father was to stuck on to change in his cartel.

If I had to think of anyone that would want to step into his
shoes, it would be Roberto's flamboyant ass. He would love

to run that shit and change it up to his liking. I had been planning on having that talk with my father in a couple of months when the time was right. With him worrying about the Golden Triangle and making sure no more hits were taken on his life. I didn't want to spring that out on him.

I moved the heavy picture frame and opened up the door that led to my chambers. Turning on the light, we walked down the steps until we stood in the middle of the floor. I loved the smell down here in Hades and welcomed it each time I stepped down here.

"I burn all of my problems down here. That's what you are going to do tonight, you gon' burn some shit and then put the past behind you. If you haven't already killed close to every nigga that violated, then I will. We can bring them niggas down here and burn their asses together." I walked to the corner of the room and grabbed the lighter fluid and my mini flamethrower.

I already had a pile of wood and papers that needed to be shredded from the syndicate that I would now burn tonight. We filed a bunch of papers every month to keep things organized. A lot of that paperwork that could incriminate me got destroyed. Excitement flowed through me, I hadn't started a fire in weeks and now I was about to let Sovereign do the honors.

I placed the flamethrower into her delicate hands and helped her balance it. I was so close to her naked flesh that I couldn't stop my dick from bricking up behind her.

"You gon' imagine all the people from the past that wronged you. That nigga Melvin gone be right in this room as soon as we capture that nigga as husband and wife. Anybody else that cross you and fuck you over can go in here too. For right now though, I want you to mentally place your past right in the middle of this room. I want you to allow the flames to hypnotize and relax you from all of the burdens you feel. This shit gone give you a fascination and gratification of having some form of relief." I stepped from behind her and poured the fluid on top of the wood and papers.

I tossed the bottle in the middle and made sure I had the fire extinguishers near to put it out when it became too much to inhale.

"If you feel yourself choking off of too much smoke then go up the stairs and back into my room. She nodded her head as I stood behind her. Her finger already on the trigger, I placed my hand on top of hers and held it down until the smell of gas hit our nose. She took the lead and let the flames from my flame thrower attack the paper and it spread out in hit the wood and coils. We both remained quiet, the fire held my attention and relaxed me at the same time.

Three minutes into watching the fire, I turned her around to face me. I looked into her eyes they look so fucking pure and innocent although I know they are far from that. I watch her pouty plump lips tremble as her eyes mist over. Picking her up off of her feet, her legs wrap around me instinctively and in one motion, I enter her snug tunnel. We both released the breaths between each other. Sovereign sighs as the fire crackles, laying her head on my broad shoulder.

I gaze at the fire unable to look away by how beautiful it looks. The feel of her hot ass silky pussy locked on my dick while watching another fire she started was probably one of the best feelings I have ever felt. I can't stop my grip from tightening underneath her ass cheeks. I push out a little from inside of her, the feeling of her hard nipple rubbing up against me, makes me push in deeper as she bites my shoulder.

My fingers drift up to her throat as her eyes roll back and she coughs from the burning fire. Not wanting to slide out of her, I squat with her still in my arms and pick up the fire extinguisher to put the fire out. I can feel my own lungs burning. I make it up the stairs with her moaning and bouncing all over my dick. Opting out of putting her down again, I leave the door to Hades opened and take her straight to my bed.

Sliding out of her is almost torture as I lay her down on my cool sheets and look at her naked body sprawled out on my silk sheets. Fuck, Sovereign had me thinking of ways to please her and make things better for her. She had me ready to prove her wrong, I wanted her hooked on me and wanted to show her what the fuck loyalty looked like.

I was a boss, a kingpin, I made grown men cry and show fear whenever or wherever I showed my face. I was able to obtain a lot of things and figure shit the fuck out. However, potentially loving someone and trying to figure them out was never something I thought about. A lot of people told me their problems and cried out in front of me. It never moved me like how Sovereign tears did.

Sovereign tears had me ready to figure some shit out for her, she had this aura that automatically made me want to become her protector. For the first time ever, I thought of ways to actually make a woman happy besides giving up this magnificent dick. All of this shit was new to me but one thing I wouldn't do was run from how I was feeling.

I was ready for whatever the fuck this was. Sovereign opened her legs exposing the prettiest pussy. Shit was obese as fuck and looked like it tasted sweet, like my favorite fruit. Her smooth sepia skin tone looked richer than chocolate. Drowning between her thick thighs and sweet essence, I inhaled and sniffed her center like my next breath of air was dependent on it.

"You need something, Sovereign?" I blew on her swollen pearl tongue and her body trembled right before me. My balls ached; my dick was hard throbbing against the silk sheets.

"You." She stated breathlessly. That's all I needed to hear before I attacked her center. The more I licked and sucked on her swollen nub the higher that ache in my dick grew to be deep inside of her. I thrusted my tongue inside of her contracting center savoring the sweet taste of her pussy, hearing her whimper and move around the bed like she was running from the pleasure that I was giving her had me on edge. Animalistic grunts and growls escaped me as I parted her thick lips and slid my finger around her clit. I rose up and pressed my lips on the side of her neck. I let my dick bump all up against her slippery pussy. Dragging my tongue along the artery of her neck, I sank my teeth deep, keeping a hold around her throat.

The moan that tore from her throat vibrated against my hand; I entered her right then in there. Watching her fist, the sheets desperately, her eyes fluttered and watered. Her dark brown nipples puckered for me. I lowered my head and grazed them and bit down just enough to watch her flinch.

"Turn over, Sovereign." I wanted my sheets to catch whatever tears that dropped from her eyes. In due time, those same tears, I planned on licking.

I rose up, giving her enough space to turn over. Her body was trembling with need.

"On your hands and knees, Sovereign." It was my turn to take control and let her feel how dominate I liked to be.

I watched her like a hawk watching its prey, I didn't want to miss shit. Her body language was talking to me in ways that I was ready to communicate back with. I watched her full breast sway as she turned and licked my lips hungrily. She pushed up on trembling arms. Ass up in the air with a perfect fucking arch in her back.

I wanted to turn on my fireplace to make her sweat more, so we could slip and slid all around this room. I'd save that for another time. I grazed her sensitive flesh then stopped at her ass, pushing a finger in, her body fought and tried to reject me. Pushing my dick deep inside of her sopping wet center, her pussy clenched at the invasion.

"Fuck, Sovereign! This my pussy, you hear me? You belong to me." That was fucking final. I didn't need for her to respond or say shit, what she thought didn't matter. She could play hard to get all she wanted to. This pussy would only know me from now on. Her body count officially started over when I entered her. She dropped her head at my words and drove back on my dick as I smacked that ass and pushed in deeper.

"This ass is mine." I slapped hard again as I declared her as being mine. I hope she knew what the fuck came with that. You couldn't just walk around with this type of pussy and expect a nigga not to act a fucking fool.

She whimpered and whined but worked that pussy on my dick like a grown ass woman was supposed to. I drove in and out that pussy with my finger in her ass just how she needed.

"Spread them legs wider, Sovereign." She didn't listen, Sovereign was to entranced by my finger, knuckle deep in her ass. My dick was hitting past her tight pussy walls. She was no longer moaning softly; she was roaring like a lioness close to reaching her peak. I stopped stroking, slamming my hand down on her left as cheek her body jolted. Fisting a hand full of hair, I repeated myself to her.

"Spread those fucking legs, Sovereign." She shifted then widened her knees, I had more access to the pussy. She moaned with a sensation, like she knew what was to come as I started to punish her pussy with her ass cheeks held captive in my hands. I had her cheeks spread far apart. Watching my dick disappear and reappear coated with her slick clear essence.

"Fuck!" I roared. Her head dropped, arms shaking, whimpering and crying out for deliverance. I was focused on the feel of her pussy fighting my dick, this shit was biting hard making it hard to even focus. Her body was gripping me tight as fuck, she fucked back the best she could, but her pussy was doing all the cursing and fucking.

The wet slaps of our bodies, the small praise that came from her mouth had my balls clenching and tightening. I was ready for a release; I sped the pace up and felt her shaking hard as hell. Harsh breaths escaped me as my heart rate increased.

"I need you, to nut all on my dick, Sovereign." I watched her arms buckle, sending her face first into the bed, her body was quivering, pussy contracting. I made her turn over, I needed to look into her eyes while she caught all of this nut. Soon as she was on her back, I got right back deep inside of her. Grabbing her hand and yanking that shit over her head. Pecking her opened lips then sliding my tongue deep inside of her mouth. We shared a nasty passionate kiss, I started back up my assault, loving the feel of her trembling body underneath.

"Breathe baby, take all of this dick." Gripping her jaw, I made her glistening eyes focus in on me. I was giving her brutal blows, purposely making sure my pelvis knocked up against her clit. I slammed home thrust after thrust. Sovereign let out a loud cry as her head fell back, I pinched those puckered nipples and enjoyed the feel of her pussy spasming on my dick.

Warmth spilled around me, an unfamiliar warmth in my chest, no words could encompass me as I filled her watching her body bounce.

"Cum, one more time on this dick, baby." She shuddered as her pussy pulsed; I dropped my head against her shoulder.

I released deep inside of her and that warmth feeling grew deeper throughout my entire body.

Turning on my back and pulling her up to my chest, our breathing was labored. My mind and body were numb as I tried to find my ability to speak.

"I know your depths, and I want you to know mine… one day Sovereign. I'm fucking hooked on you. I'm not sex high either. I'm saying this shit sober as fuck. You are mine, and I'll burn Cali and Mexico down behind you baby." She sighed and smiled lazily as she threw her leg over mine.

"I'm hooked on you too, Malice. Your mine… any bitch you was fucking, is done with now. Make sure you let Kenya know before I have to."

I nodded my head and closed my eyes as our breathing slowed and we both drifted off to a peaceful sleep. Looks like this was no longer business. It was hell of personal, anyone stepping in the way of what Sovereign, and I was building would be burned alive. She was like a special drug that people gave up their self-dignity for. She was meant to be with a nigga like me.

SOULFUL HURTZ

$\mathcal{I}$ hated the rain, but that was California weather for you. The rain always seemed to make me think of my problems a little harder. A strong feeling of hopelessness was taking over my whole mind. I was fighting through this shit the best way I knew how. I thought having money and being able to finally provide without worrying about feeding my sisters would help out majorly and it did. Mentally though, it did nothing for me.

I was having a hard time getting my sisters on board with not having our mom around. I didn't expect them to understand, I just thought that it wouldn't be this hard. Every day Luv acted out and popped off at the mouth asking about Antoinette.

I was already dealing with a lack of concentration when it came to the street shit. I didn't know much about dealing with a young ass kid that had a smart-ass mouth. I was trying to teach Luv and Passion about respect, but they saw me as being their big brother. Passion stayed quiet a lot and would randomly ask questions about that night. The night of me finding her and my mom at that damn park.

That night couldn't leave my brain, it stuck to me more than the two bodies I caught. I had a persistent feeling of sadness and I lost interest in everything. I didn't know how to cope with that shit. Seeing my mom in that particular state had me tossing and turning every fucking night. I didn't get much sleep and when I looked over in the mirror it was obvious that I was starting to drop pounds from the lack of having an appetite.

I wanted to see Jocelyn, but I refused to place my dead weight on her. We were both eighteen but to me she had a happier life ahead of her. I decided to let her go so she wouldn't constantly look at me with sad judgmental eyes. I hadn't been to school in months and was better off without that shit.

The way that I had been feeling these days was dangerous. It's like I had the urge to kill again and find a way to release all this pent-up pain and anger.

On top of that, I still hadn't heard or saw Sovereign. Bundy and I were maintaining things good as fuck. Since I wasn't attending school, I ate, slept and bled the block. I stayed on top of niggas and made sure the count was right each week. If a nigga got mouthy with me, I practically broke his face in half.

Days of taking disrespect was over with, I stood on everything I said and meant that shit. That shit with Clapback and Murk'um had me looking at muthafuckas sideways. Each week when it was meeting time, I arrived two hours early like today. I got out and sat in the back seat of my car behind tinted windows and just observed. Most of them never even noticed my car parked on the street because they pulled right in and stood out in the parking lot talking and laughing with no cares in the world.

I would hot box my back seat and watch, just to see if I

would catch some shit that was unusual. By the time everybody went inside, I was the last man walking in.

Taking my eyes away from the gang, my cell phone alerted me that my sister's school was calling. I already knew that it had nothing to do with Passion. They were most likely calling about Luv's ass. I answered on the third ring and was greeted by the principal.

"Hello, this is Mrs. Wilbern calling from Eastside elementary." I watched three black Cadillac Escalades pull into the warehouse parking lot and sat up some to focus on who the fuck it was. Opening up the middle console, I reached in and pulled my gun out and sat it in my lap.

"I'm sorry Mrs. Wilbern, I'm in the middle of a meeting. Is everything okay?" I tried to sound proper as fuck but was starting to fail at doing so. In a couple of seconds, I would probably be hanging up in this bitch face to go into action once I saw who was all hopping out of these unknown cars.

"Luv has been suspended for fighting and using profanity towards her substitute teacher. I truly thinks she needs an I.E.P like we discussed." I shook my head no, like she could see me. My nose was practically glued to my back seat window watching closely. I heard Mrs. Wilbern clear her throat and then I finally responded to her.

"Luv don't need a I.E.P she's not dumb. She passes all her test; she's reading and writing plus doing math at the right grade level. I will talk to her and put her on punishment." I tried to reassure her but that wasn't good enough for the principal.

"Yes, Soulful… I understand, however, an I.E.P can grant her a behavioral counselor. Someone to pull her out of class a couple of times a day so that she can keep busy and focus more on finishing her class assignments. Luv grades are being affected because she has loud outbursts and argues with other students while the teacher is trying her very best to control the class setting."

Two niggas stepped out of the third black truck and walked towards the Escalade that was parked in the middle of both trucks. They separated and looked around like they were peeping the scene.

"I've decided to let her finish the rest of the school day. She will be suspended for two days." Now that shit pissed me off, I planned on getting on Luv's ass when I picked her up today from school. She couldn't go to daycare because they expelled her, so now her ass had to come straight home from school.

"Okay thanks, Mrs. Wilbern." I hung up and watched Inferno step out the truck looking like the devil in all red. The same nigga that gave me the address and keys to the condo in the city of Torrance stepped out of the driver side of the first Escalade. The next person that exited the passenger side was that pretty boy ass nigga named Killa.

I don't know why I swallowed down out of nervousness, but when my eyes landed on Inferno helping Queen out of the backseat, I calmed seeing her face.

Queen's hair looked wild and curly hanging above her round ass. Balenciaga shades covered her eyes. She rocked a teal blue crew neck Balmain shirt with a pair of white joggers. On her feet were teal blue low top chucks. She was dressed down but still looked like money. I could see the diamond stud earrings shining like her glossed up lips from a distance. The ice on her neck gleamed even though it was raining. Inferno took the umbrella from Big B's hand and opened it. Placing it above Queen's head like the queen she was.

Together they looked like wealth, Inferno leaned down and whispered something in Queen's ear and she nodded her head and smiled up at him. The gesture was weird as hell, because I never witnessed Queen smile at a nigga. Inferno grabbed her hand, and they walked toward the entrance. This meeting was going to be very interesting.

Grabbing my black Nike hoodie, I put it on and stepped out of my car. Walking across the street, I made it into the parking lot and walked past the two big security niggas that stood with their hands folded in front of them.

I entered the front of the warehouse and was surprised at the three sixty on the inside. Instead of folding tables being in the center of the room, Queen replaced them and had the front of the warehouse looking like a big office space. She had about forty comfortable office chairs still wrapped in plastic. I could see the second level from where I stood. Big boxes that looked to be shipped out sat stacked neatly up there. I also notice her office on the second floor that had her name stamped on the door.

"Glad everyone is here and on time. This is officially F.Y.F's new headquarters." Her voice echoed in the room as she pulled her glasses from her face. This was my first time seeing the face tattoos and also seeing her face bare of any makeup.

I took a seat at the end of the table and locked eyes with Inferno. He stood behind Queen and his men stood behind him.

"A lot has happened." She paused from talking as Bundy approached her with a blunt. She smiled up at him as Inferno frowned. Before she could open her mouth to take the blunt between her lips, Inferno snatched it from Bundy and balled that shit up. He tossed it like a paper written with errors across the room.

Big B stepped to the side of him, but Inferno shook his head no, and then sneered.

"I hate to cut my wife off, but I'm only going to say this shit once. So that you niggas and females can save yourselves from dying." He looked over the entire room with an icy glare.

"Disrespect will be matched with death. If you have never known what it feels like to be burned alive, then I know muthafuckas better show respect at all times." He turned towards Bundy and reached for the top button of his Polo shirt. He buttoned that shit up and dusted off imaginary dust from his shirt.

"Tighten up and tuck your feelings, boy. Don't ever disrespect me again." He moved away and turned towards Queen. He leaned down and pecked her lips, then traced her lips to get rid of any lip gloss that smeared the rim of her lips. When he was done, he stepped behind her and eyed only Bundy.

I felt for Bundy, everyone in this room knew that he was in love with Queen. Big B handed Inferno a blunt along with a mini torch. He then placed the blunt between Queen's lips then sparked it for her. She took a deep pull with a satisfied look on her face.

"Things are changing, I made a promise that the gang would eat better. I also said that when the time is right... I will explain things to you all, so here I am ready to explain only enough to give you all a better understanding." She paused and took another long pull, placing the lit blunt on the table. Queen folded her hands in front of her with her elbows placed on the table. It looked like she was battling with her first set of words.

"To those of you that don't know, this is Inferno my husband. He is the head of a syndicate that stretches throughout the United States. Good connections and more power. While our marriage wasn't quite an idea, it is solid and F.Y.F plus the syndicate is now business partners. We are no longer nickel and diming it. This means more money and stepping it the fuck up. New positions will be in place for all of you. Bundy and Teddy will meet with you all in two days to explain your new position. You can't be out in the streets moving recklessly are drawing attention to what we now have." Queen picked up her blunt and ashed it on the new oakwood table and took another hit.

"Greed will not get you far, disloyalty will get you killed..."

"So all that talk about never getting down with these weird ass niggas was just for show? Where the fuck is Clap-back? Seem like everything she was saying was true. This shit not gang! We live and breathe the streets now you trying to push some other shit on us like we all pose to get in line." Peep stood tall, his face was red, and tension started to swarm throughout the room as everyone else remained quiet.

Queen broke the silence by laughing softly. Inferno turned to look at Big B and without uttering a word, Big B handed Inferno his flamethrower. Killa stood off to the side chuckling watching the scene unfold.

Big B approached Peep and Peep already started pulling his pants up to square up with Big B. It was obvious that Peep was no match for Big B. Big B knew it too because he smiled, reaching into his back pocket pulling out a clear water bottle with liquid swishing around inside. Unscrewing the top, Big B threw the liquid all over Peep's face. He instantly screeched and rubbed his eyes to try to see clear but it was too late.

Inferno pulled the trigger, the flamethrower ignited flames toward Peep. The fire instantly caught onto the liquid and set Peep's face and chest on fire. He screamed out in agony and ran into shit as people moved out of the way.

"Somebody get this nigga a chair, it's time to melt in

peace nigga." Inferno watched him like he was more infatuated with the fire. By now it was too late for Peep to take a seat, his screams had turned into whimpers. His body started to shake and convulse on the ground as Big B added more liquid like you do on the grill to keep the coils burning.

Inferno stood with a Cuban cigar, he bent down close to Peep's body and used the fire to light the end of his cigar. He took a deep hit and then stood close to Peep's burning fire. It was like he was now captivated, and his attention had been diverted.

"Unfortunately, Clapback and Murk'um is no longer with us. They had to retire early from the gang. From here on out their names are not to be mentioned. Don't question the moves that I am making for the gang that I created. I can look at every single one of you and see the difference. I smell money and see full bellies. Y'all been eating good as fuck, so why try to starve yourselves by thinking stupidly?" Queen had a look of determination planted in her eyes.

"Now if anyone of you feel like it's too much then by all means, walk out that door." She sat back in her chair as we all looked around. The first person to stand was Lady Minks, she stayed running her mouth and was close with Clapback. I didn't trust her much anyway and had my eyes glued to her at all times, especially since Clapback tried to set me up.

Lady Minks walked towards the exit and Queen pulled her gun, calling Minks' name. Minks turned around with her eyes glued to Queen.

"You always talked to much bitch. When you get to hell, tell that nigga Murk'um that when it's my time to go there too, that I'm gone see about his treacherous ass." She emptied the clip with good ass aim. The first shot hit Minks in the stomach, she was still standing even after the second shot to the chest. The third shot went right between her eyes sending her to the ground. Queen stood and walked over to her and pressed the trigger a couple more times.

"Stupid bitch." Placing her hands on her thick hips she sauntered close to Peep and spit on him. Big B was now holding an extinguisher putting the burning fire out. The room smelled like burnt flesh and hair.

"This meeting is over. Teddy stay back so we can talk." I nodded my head and watched men enter the warehouse. I assumed they were with Inferno; they were the same men that came and got Clapback and Murk'um from my house. Once the warehouse was cleared out Queen took a seat while Inferno and his men stood by the exit talking.

"My apologies that it took so long Teddy. A lot of heavy shit was going down and at the time, I wasn't out here. I don't have any hard feelings toward you, you did what you were supposed to. Just for that and all your loyalty I want you to remain lieutenant and stick this shit out. I know yo ass ain't been to school, you know I don't like that shit. You only got a couple of months to finish. Then I am willing and open to letting you decide if you still want to be down."

"I'm always gon' be down." I made sure to give her proper eye contact to let her know how serious I was. Outside of my sisters, Queen was there and was like family. She came through for me when I was at my breaking point.

"I know you are, but I want to give you options Teddy. If you want to live a normal life and not look over your shoulders and worry about the type of bullshit that Clapback did to you. I'm an understanding and selfless person. I know what it feels like to not have many options and to sacrifice some shit to make sure there is food on the table. I wouldn't feel any type of way about letting you be free Teddy. We will always be tight." She patted her chest to solidify that.

"I know, and I appreciate you, Queen. My sister and the

gang is all I got. I want next level type of shit, I ain't going nowhere." My mom was selfish and didn't think about her kids. I wanted more for my sisters. I didn't want them growing up limited, I didn't want college are none of that other shit that kids my age wanted. All I wanted was peace for my sisters. I didn't want them growing up, becoming my age, and feeling so depressed. Working with Queen was like being groomed into becoming a real man.

That was some shit I truly needed to be able to survive the storm. I'd worked off my debt and this wasn't the first time Queen offered to get me a legit job.

"I got a good job for you once you hit twenty-one if you don't want to be wrapped into the drugs and being exposed to a lot. You can have a seat on the board of my new corporation that I'm building from the ground up. You got a couple of years to think it through, in the meantime, keep doing what you doing. I see a lot of potential in you." Inferno said as he held his hand out for me to shake. I shook his hand and thanked him for giving me and my sisters a place to stay. As bad as I wanted to stay back and talk some more I couldn't because I had to get the girls from school.

"Get back in school nigga, I want you over shipping now too. More money for you and the family. Also, take your full cut, you have only been taking five bands when I told you its ten now. Never cut yourself short of some shit that's owed to you. I will be seeing you tomorrow so I can tell you and Bundy about the new positions that y'all will be giving to the rest of the gang." I nodded my head and stood up feeling good about everything.

"Watch Bundy, a scorn man would do just about anything to get what he wants." Inferno looked at Queen but was talking directly to me.

"I got you." I made my way over to Queen. She stood up and hugged me then handed me a heavy envelope. "For your troubles with Clapback." She smiled at me. My chest tightened because I was now starting to have more money than I ever imagined. Thanking her once more I walked out of the warehouse feeling the depression and heavy weights that weighed me down slip away.

I pulled into the parent pickup area and waited for my sisters to walk out the gate from school. The rain in Cali made people drive crazy as hell. I could hear vehicles beeping for their kids and some parents standing out by the gate eager as hell to see their kids. Luv and Passion walked out the gate side by side.

Luv had a mug on her face, and her hair was all over her damn head, indicating that she indeed had a fight today. It was easier said than done with raising the girls. I tried to be a good father figure but also have the kind of relationship to where they could feel open enough to express themselves to me.

Passion got in the front seat today, when she normally would ride in the backseat and let Luv take the front since she was the oldest. Today, Luv's energy could be felt. She had a bad attitude and already had a look on her face like she was ready for me to get on her case.

"Can you take me to go see about my momma?" She looked out the window as I pulled off from the curb.

"I don't know where Ma is, Luv. Let's talk about you fighting and acting like you don't got sense while at school." I redirected the conversation. I was feeling good after my meeting with Queen and didn't want to ruin how I was feeling bringing up my mom.

"Lia kept talking stuff, so I beat her ass." She rolled her little frail neck, and I shook my head at her bad ass.

57

"Watch yo mouth Luv." I warned and turned the radio down. "You think I like getting calls from the principal about you not being able to control yourself?" I looked at her pretty face through the mirror and she frowned up.

"I'll do better if you just let me see about my mom! You deserting her and acting like you our damn daddy!" I merged to the left of the road and pulled over in front of Wendy's then put my hazards on. Turning in my seat, I looked over at Luv. I really was tempted to whoop her ass.

"Keep talking to me disrespectfully Luv and I'ma beat yo ass. I ain't desert momma! She deserted us and almost got Passion hurt real bad from those drugs." I let that slip from anger and regret even saying it. I could hear Passion sniffling and already knew she was crying.

"I'm going to find my momma!" She snatched at the back door and then hopped out. She took off running down the damn street. I sighed with a heavy heart, putting on my hazards, I hopped out and started running after her. Once I caught up with her, she kicked and screamed in my arms. Hearing her scream at the top of her lungs saying how much she hated me, broke my fucking heart. I didn't know what to do to make this shit better, I would never give up on Luv, but she was making this shit harder than it needed to be.

"Chill Luv, I promise I will go find momma and try to get her some help. You making things hard when I'm just doing the best I can to protect y'all from disappointment and hurt." I turned the hazards off and pulled back into traffic. I opted out of turning the radio up, I was gone buy them some pizza and take my ass home so I could smoke the biggest blunt possible.

I worried about my mom just as much as the girls. I wondered if she went and tried to get help after her getting raped in beat in front of her own daughter. In my mind that should have been all it took for her to go get cleaned up.

That same dreadful feeling was starting to come over me again. I had an envelope full of money and backpay coming my way from the money I didn't take from my cut with Queen. Yet I still found it hard to find my own happiness even if it was for just one damn day.

Money didn't buy happiness, and I now knew this to be true. So, for the sake of my sisters, I would push my anger and resentment to the side and find my mother. Luv and Passion were too young right now to understand and see things the way that I did. Disciplining was also something that I didn't know shit about. I could threaten Luv all day but she and I both knew that I would never lay a finger on her.

KENYA MONROE

*T*hree months later….
I sat at an upscale hookah lounge watching a bunch of people laugh and dance. I wished just for a moment that I could steal some of their joy and feel just how they were feeling. I remember when I used to be happy and ready to conquer the world. Lately I've been so caught up on trying to desperately find ways for Inferno to notice me.

I was still seething when I tried to make a deposit two months ago and the private bank had notified me that my name had been taken off of all accounts. I felt like Inferno snatched something intimate away from me. Depositing large amounts of money made me feel like he trusted me and now it seemed like that bitch Queen had come along and was changing things to her liking.

In meetings, Inferno barely even looked at me. I gave reports, and even put out new ideas and all he did was nod and stare at his phone hard. He still would come by the condo some days for us to work on paperwork for the syndicate. He'd eat my food and talk like we were still friends. I would wait for him to ask me if I needed something, but even those words that I used to long to hear didn't escape his lips.

There was no spending the night, or me working in his library at his home and sleeping in the room that he had designated for just me. I was trying my hardest to keep my cool, but it was becoming harder than ever. It was starting to feel like he was suffocating me with just the distance that he created. When I asked him last week was everything okay, he looked at me for a long time then chuckled. A chuckle that made me feel like I was pitiful. I felt firsthand embarrassment when I spoke up and tried to even express myself.

"This better be good bitch, I canceled my late-night dick session just to see what your dangerously in love ass want." I watched Mi'elle sit down like she was the queen of England. Looking at her then back at me would make everyone wonder why the fuck was he so caught up in that girl Queen. I couldn't lie and say Queen was ugly, she was the true definition of beautiful for a big girl.

Standing next to Mi'elle and I, she couldn't hold a candle to us. We were bad bitches up and down. From our faces to our perfectly sculpted bodies, I just didn't see what Inferno's infatuation came from with this girl.

Mi'elle lifted her hand in the air and that's when I saw a fresh tattoo of flames, followed by Inferno's name. She waved a waitress over to our table and looked at me and gave me a sinister smile. I rolled my eyes because I wish I was bold enough to do some shit like that. If I up and tatted Inferno's name he'd probably do something drastic like cut me off.

"He's in love." It pained me to say it, so I quickly looked away, trying to blink back tears. I couldn't stand Mi'elle but over the years, I learned to accept her crazy ass.

"Aww, and let me guess… You over there hurt and shit." She rolled her eyes and gave her attention to the waitress.

Once she placed her order, I picked up the napkin and dabbed the corners of my eyes.

"That doesn't bother you?" I asked, getting annoyed with the fact that I even called her to sit with me. Truth was, I felt like she was the only person that would understand how I felt. We basically shared the same dick. Mi'elle has done some crazy things. In my eyes, Inferno should have cut her off after she faked like she was pregnant.

"Hell no, I know that my pussy is top tier, and my head is even better. I don't bother the nigga, and when he bothers me. I make sure to soak this kitty in vinegar so it's as tight as it was the last time he slid in." She did a little dance in her seat and smiled. I gave her a look of disgust not believing that she was actually okay with Inferno falling in love.

"After the whole baby thing, and him showing me how he really felt about me. I found me other dick to bounce on. Good paid dick to be exact. I love Inferno and would love to be his trophy wife, but I can't put a stop to finding my real husband by waiting on him. Men like him is too powerful for they own good. They have all the money in the world, so their options are endless. I'm not about to sit up and cry myself to sleep at night, lose most of my beauty by not getting any sleep. I just can't do that shit. See, that's why he always call me first. He knows that you are a needy bitch ready to scrub his mansions floors with a toothbrush just to get his damn attention." She shook her head and opened her Chanel bag to retrieve her vape.

"I'm not saying it to hurt your feelings, Kenya. I mean, I don't care for your uppity ass, but I get how you feel. I used to feel like that the first couple of years." She looked off at nothing in particular getting serious. "I'm still in love with Malice my damn self, everything about that man is fire as fuck. I just was able to accept that I ain't the woman for him and you need to accept it too. If we were the women for him, it wouldn't be two of us and one of her."

"You say that like she is above us." I hissed, getting pissed how she put it.

"Bitch, she is that niggas wife. Don't say shit about it being business either. I brought one of my baddest bitches over a couple of months ago for his birthday in Mexico. Nigga flew me out and everything. His wife walked in that room while we were all fucking. She walked out all calm and shit, and in my head, I figured, yea, this some arranged shit. When I was getting ready to leave, she set one of the niggas favorite cars on fire and he didn't do shit about it. If that was us, we would be dead. So, yes bitch… that separates us from her." She thanked the waitress for her drink and took a slow sip.

"Kenya, you gotta find you some good dick to occupy your mind from Inferno. You can't keep doing this to yourself. Look at you, you called me out of all people, and you know we don't like each other." We both giggled at that. I couldn't stand Mi'elle, she was ghetto and very classless about herself. I never considered screwing someone else besides Inferno. It felt like cheating, and I didn't want him viewing me as a whore either. The idea didn't sound too bad though. I desperately needed a distraction.

"What if we both offer ourselves to him exclusively? Like a relationship type of thing." Mi'elle raised her brows at that like she was thinking about it.

"I do like licking some good pussy. It looks like you taste good as fuck too. I don't know bitch; I'll think about it. In the meantime, go find yourself some side dick to jump on. I can't exclusively be with no nigga unless he trying to marry me. Your idea sounds good because Inferno is paid, but that doesn't mean he would settle for just us. I'm keeping my options open. Now go mingle like I'm about to go do. Unlike you, I ain't on that niggas payroll so this drink is on you." She smiled and stood up, fixing her tight-ass leather mini skirt. She strutted off like she was on the runway and mixed into the crowd.

What a bitch, I thought to myself as I sighed extra hard. I thought back to what she said and cringed. Out of all the years of being involved with Inferno, I never pictured myself with another man. Inferno was everything to me, somewhere down the line, I got caught up in all of him. I yearned for him and loved everything there was to him.

I could look at other men and see that they were handsome and had some form of sex appeal. My mind and body just didn't view them like I viewed Inferno. I nursed my drink for a few more minutes until a tall brawny guy walked right up to my table. His peanut butter smooth skin is what got my attention first, followed by his cologne.

"I see you sitting alone, and, since I came alone… I was wondering if you could use some extra company." I shrugged and he took a seat. For a while, we both just sat in comfortable silence.

"Who broke your heart?" He placed his elbows on the table and stared me deep in the eyes. His aura was kind of comforting and I felt like I could open up to him. He was dressed nicely, with a simple Ralph Lauren, a white shirt, and blue denim jeans.

"I broke my own heart, I guess. I can't really blame the love of my life, since he made things clear from the jump, you know?" I offered him a small sad smile. I wasn't going to sit here and bash Inferno when it was really my fault. I became so caught up in the feeling Inferno gave me that I desperately wanted him to feel exactly how I felt about him.

I mean why wouldn't he feel a certain way about me? I

was beautiful, and in shape and I handled business well for him. I knew my sex had to be amazing as well since he kept coming back to me. I just was having a hard time making him fall in love with me, which ached me the most.

"I guess that's some shit we got in common." His deep voice caught my attention, my eyes met his and we just stared at each other for a couple of seconds. I gave him the floor to speak because now I was curious.

"I'm in love with a woman, that has moved on. So, I'm at the stage of forcing myself to fall out of love with her and that shit is very hard." His jaws clenched tight; anger crossed his handsome face as he looked up at the waitress. I put a request in for a hookah with watermelon flavor and a lemon drop. He told her he wanted five shots of Remy, no chaser.

Once the waitress was out of sight, we focused back on each other.

"What makes you love her?" Maybe his situation could possibly make me feel a little better about my own crazy situation and how I felt about Inferno. It felt good to know that I wasn't the only one that had fallen deep in love into a one-sided relationship.

"It was her strength first, all of the things she had been through. Her ability to snap back in any situation. She's a true hustler and it's a turn-on when you come from the streets. To people on the outside looking in, she appears heartless as fuck. When you get to really know her, she's caring, and she puts people around her in the position to thrive. Then there's her raw beauty, I can't really explain that shit. She is physically beautiful, but her personality makes her astounding. We connected one night, but because of her past, she quickly shut the shit down. Since that night, I've been trying to figure out ways to get that connection back. It's gone and she has made it clear that she will never view me as anything more than what I am now."

His eyes were now glossy, and I felt myself getting emotional. I wished Inferno could speak and feel that way about me.

"Why give up? Aren't you loyal to her?" I asked seriously. He let out a deep chuckle and shook his head no.

"Business-wise, I will always be loyal. We work together. As far as me with other women no. I never even got a chance to see what her pussy smells like. I just fell in love with the woman she is. I don' imagined her carrying my kids and wearing a ring from me. Sometimes we allow our hearts to control our rightful minds. You can't force something that wasn't meant to be, even if you feel like it suppose to be." The waiter walked up with another waiter. They sat our items down and he took down two shots.

"You should keep trying." I encouraged him, I didn't see myself giving up on Inferno. I felt like one day, he would finally see that I was truly meant for him.

"No, I give up. She's married and I can see how she looks at him. I don't ever recall her looking at any other nigga this particular way. Besides… I love her so much and care about her happiness that I am willing to set my selfish desires to the side and let her be in love. I won't interfere with what she has because she deserves it." He looked off and picked up his third shot.

"I just know that if this nigga harm a single hair on her head, then I'm going to be ready to go to war behind her. I'll also be there to pick up all the broken pieces to her heart. I just feel like her husband is actually meant for her." He took the drink down and slammed the glass down like he hated what he just said.

"Wow, that's really deep. I'm so in love with this guy that

I have been involved with for years now that, I don't know how to let go and just live." I admitted. My whole world revolved around Inferno. It was sickening when I really sat back and thought about the whole situation. I just couldn't help how I felt.

"I'm sorry, I guess we are both being rude. My name is Kenya, and yours?" I realized I just allowed this stranger at my table without us both introducing each other.

"You good, I saw you sitting here and just felt connected to you and some type of way that I can't really explain. My name is Bundy. Kenya, whoever this man is, is a fool to not see this raw beauty right in front of him. Tell me more about yourself, if you don't mind."

I smiled and felt refreshed, it felt even better that I was able to sit back and talk to a man all about how I felt.

SOVEREIGN

I watched Inferno cross his arms over his chest, his eyes never faltered as he looked my Abuela directly in the eyes. His butterscotch smooth skin looked radiant as hell. Malice's prominent blue eyes lit up the entire room. I watched his every movement down to him licking those cinnamon pinkish lips then diverting his eyes towards me every couple of seconds and winking.

BY HIS BODY LANGUAGE, and him looking down at his watch, I could tell that he would rather be anywhere than here. These past couple of months had been a big ass blur for me especially. I constantly came back and forth from Cali to Mexico to conduct business so much that I hadn't been able to really enjoy all the money that I had been making.

THEN THERE WAS MY MARRIAGE, a marriage that started off strictly business but ended up having so much passion. I hadn't pressed Malice about shit because I didn't know which direction we were headed. What confused me even more was that he hadn't touched me in three months. Leaving me to wonder who this nigga was dropping dick off in.

I ALREADY MADE up my mind that I wasn't willing to share the type of dick he was packing with anyone else. So, I hope he was finding something safe to do, like keeping them balls heavy until it was time to release all the pint up nut inside of me.

"SOVEREIGN? ARE YOU OKAY MIJO?" I quickly snapped out of my thoughts and licked my glossed-up lips and looked at my Abuela.

"YES, I was just thinking about some business that I needed to tend to." I ran my hands through my silky tresses and instantly missed my wild curls. I had my hair bone straight because it was more tamable this way. I missed the extra volume and the bounce the curls had given me.

I was trying to stay focused but seeing that flamethrower leaning up against Malice leg. Plus, seeing his handsome ass face, I realized my hormones were going crazy. I desperately needed to get fucking laid.

"YOU NEED SOMETHING SOVEREIGN?" He sneered, as his eyes smiled at me my stomach tightened because he knew exactly what I needed. How the fuck could anyone stay focused near this fine ass man. I tried to focus on something imperfect on his face, like the burn mark on his up cheek and the other burn mark that traced his jawline leaving a dark mark. That didn't work because now I was picturing myself licking all around the shit.

WHAT THE FUCK was wrong with me?

"SOVEREIGN?" I blinked my eyes, and this man was down on one knee between my thick thighs like we were the only ones in this hot ass office. "I asked you, if you needed something?" I wanted to slap that cocky ass smirk off his face. I slowly stood up, purposely putting my pussy print in his face. Looking down at his long curly lashes, I looked up at my Abuela. Fucking, bitch.

I COULDN'T STAND the sight of her. I was starting to think that this bitch was working with Melvin. She hadn't kept her end of the bargain and that was leading me right to that nigga. Since Malice and I took over as the leaders of the cartel, the numbers had run up and shit was going very well. So well that my presence wasn't even really needed.

THE MEN that worked for the Martinez cartel had showed me the utmost respect. Every transaction and new detail that I had added to this shit was multiplying by triples. It was hard as hell faking the funk knowing everything my Abuela had done. The permanent pain she caused my family. It was the mere reason why I appreciated Malice sitting in with me, each time I had to meet with her.

. . .

IT KEPT me from putting a bullet between her fucking eyes. It was too soon, I needed shit to be in my hands fully including the cartel. I already planned on killing her ass once I closed up all other loose ends. I would put someone trustable in place of the Martinez cartel and still be considered the head of it all while I controlled things in Cali. I couldn't just up and kill her and the other heads of cartels in Mexico would start looking at both of our cartels funny.

MALICE STOOD to his feet and stroked his beard with a knowing look of what I needed.

"MY APOLOGIES, MIGUELLA." Malice spoke, by his raspy deep broken voice, I could tell that he had been yelling or he had to be catching a cold. Then the thought came to my mind, that his crazy ass had probably been in hades burning shit and the smoke and ashes fucked up his throat.

"I HAVEN'T SEEN my wife in a while, and I think she needs a talk with me. We can resume this meeting tomorrow evening." Abuela simply nodded her head and smiled gracefully.

"SI, it's good to see ju two getting along." Malice never turned to acknowledge her as he simply enclosed my hand with his rugged hand and led me out the room. We walked through my Abuela's house quietly and out to the Cadillac Escalade that awaited us.

· · ·

HE HELPED me inside of the car and got in after me. When the car took off driving, I looked directly at him. Malice rocked a tan Dickies button up shirt and shorts. He left the shirt unbuttoned showing off his chiseled defined chest. The iced-out Jesus piece shined and blinded me at the same time.

"WHO YOU BEEN FUCKING?" He offered an amused look then chuckled lowly. He threaded a hand through his short curls and shrugged his shoulders. He was trying to taunt me, and it was pissing me off. I ain't never fixed my mouth to ask a nigga where his dick had been, yet here I sat in front of Malice ready to do some crazy shit if he gave me the wrong damn answer.

"I BEEN FUCKING THIS MONEY, Sovereign. Who you been fuckin on?" He gritted at the last question he asked and that caused me to smile inwardly but I maintained a neutral facial expression.

"I GUESS I BEEN FUCKING SOMETHING." I smirked as he sat up and scooted close to me until his woodsy smell invaded my nose.

"FUCK YOU MEAN, SOVEREIGN?" He grabbed me by the throat. That sharp pinky nail tapped on the spot that left a mark from the time he penetrated my neck with that sharp ass nail.

. . .

"WHAT I MEAN IS PULL the dick and balls out now." I eyed him never blinking. In my mind, I couldn't believe what I was getting ready to do but I was determined as hell. He released my neck and looked down at his crotch. Chuckling like what I had asked was funny, but I kept a straight ass face.

"YOU MUST BE ready to suck this shit. I don't pull my dick out unless I'm about to take a piss, clean it or get it fucked and sucked on, baby." His words had me wetter than water itself.

"I DON'T SUCK DICK, never have, never will. Pull the dick out Malice."

"YOU DON'T SUCK DICK?" He tilted his head and looked at me like I was crazy. Even the driver grunted a little and cleared his throat to play shit off.

"NO, I'm too pretty to have my lips wrapped around a dick." I cast my eyes down to the crotch of his pants. His dick had gotten hard, just from me admitting to not sucking dick.

"SOVEREIGN, my dick healthy as fuck. Sucking this muthafucca will have that pussy convulsing for a nigga." He licked his sexy ass lips. I looked out the window to see just where we were. I was ready to get to our destination so I could take Malice fine ass down. My nipples ached and I desperately wanted to feel him deep inside of me.

73

. . .

"I DON'T SUCK DICK, Malice... that's final. Now pull the dick out." I nodded my head towards his dick, and he slowly unbuttoned his pants. Pushing his body upward he pulled his pants down. Satisfaction hit me hard that he was actually listening to what I was telling his hardheaded ass. I watched his dick spring out and stand up at attention.

"YO MOUTH WATERING like you want to suck it now." Indeed, the sight of his dick had my mouth watering. His thick mushroom tip was starting to leak precum, the shape of his dick and how wide and long it was had my walls contracting. I rubbed my hands together to warm them up and slid them right underneath his ball sack.

"WHAT THE FUCK YOU DOING, SOVEREIGN?" His brows damn near touched his hair line as I juggled his balls and one hand checking to see how heavy they were. His balls were tight like he hadn't released in a long ass time. Just to fuck with him some more, I lowered my head until I was close enough to feel the warmness of his dick and inhaled.

TURNING my head so my nose wouldn't graze the precum leaking from the tip of his dick, I let my lips tickle the shaft of his dick. Sticking my tongue out, I tasted his skin, hearing him take a deep breath had me ready to try sucking dick for the first time.

. . .

74

"GET THE FUCK UP SOVEREIGN. I don't do that teasing shit." He was breathing hard as hell, and it had my insides jumping. I giggled and licked the vein leading down to his balls. Malice smelled like fresh soap; the skin of his dick wasn't salty either. I was thrilled and even more excited that I even went this far with my mouth right on his dick.

"I SAID GET UP, for I have you sucking dick, girl."

* * *

MALICE STOOD up and I followed suit, testing the waters. He leaned down to press his lips up against mine. Grabbing me around the waist, he took steps backwards as he pushed his tongue deep inside of my mouth. Not caring about our surroundings, I closed my eyes and allowed my tongue to wrestle with his. The double doors to the front of his house opened and he picked me up right off my feet.

THE COOL AC hit my face as I wrapped my arms around him and simpered at the feel of his huge hands massaging my ass. Nibbling on my bottom lip he whispered against my lips.

"IF YOU DON'T WANT me sharing this dick, then prove it right now. You got my dick out and exposed, yet I don't feel that hot ass pussy bouncing up and down on my shit." He reached between my thighs and ripped my panties. I was happy that I wore my silk Versace bondage dress. Right now, I was burning up with anxiousness to feel him inside of me.

. . .

"YOU WANT this dick to be exclusively yours, Sovereign?" He pushed deep inside of me and gripped my ass cheeks tight. Pulling them apart, I could feel him deeper as I fought to catch my breath. Heading towards the steps my nipples grew hard against the silk fabric.

"FUCK ME, MALICE." I moaned as I buried my face into the nook of his neck. Taking his flesh between my teeth I bit down hard and rotated my hips to meet each thrust he delivered.

"TELL me this dick belong to you, baby. I swear I'll fuck the lining out of this pussy all damn night girl." He started towards the steps and didn't stroke my pussy like I wanted him to. So, I caved in and admitted to wanting his dick for only me.

"THIS MY DICK." I stated out of breath clinging to him.

"MMHMM, you right as fuck baby. Ain't no other pussy gripping this dick like this pussy biting." He plunged deeper inside of me as he took the steps by two, amazing me with his upper body strength. Malice was medium built, his body was beautifully sculpted, solid and hard. When we got to the last step, I could feel my juices gushing out of me with each stroke he delivered.

· · ·

I FROWNED HEARING feminine moans coming from down the hallway. Malice heard that shit too because he slid out of me fast and pulled his gun from the back of his pants. It was my first time actually seeing his ass with a damn gun. Standing on wobbly legs, I bent down and pulled my gun from my Versace Aevitias platform boots. Malice raised a brow and smirked as I followed closely behind him.

I WAS ready to kill somebody just for fucking up the lethal strokes that Malice had been delivering since we took to the steps.

"OH, FUCK PAPI! RIGHT THERE!!!" A female hollered at the top of her lungs like somebody was killing her pussy. You could hear how wet she was the closer we got to the door. Wasting no time, Malice pushed the door open, and my eyes got wide as hell.

ROBERTO WAS between a mixed looking chick thigh fucking her rough. I bit my bottom lip to keep from laughing so hard because he had a pink Gucci scarf wrapped around his neck. He rotated his hips like he was getting ready to twerk. Each time he pushed inside of the woman, his ass cheeks jiggled.

"FUCK! MAMMA MIAAAAA! SQUEEZE TIGHTER." He leaned down and bit her pink pebble nipple. I blinked my eyes fast to make sure what I was seeing was real. Malice used the tip of the gun to scratch his forehead.

. . .

"ROBERTO?" I mumbled, grabbing both of their attention. Roberto turned and looked at me and winked with a Cheshire smile on his face.

"WHAT CHICA! I told you I was delivert." He looked at Malice and smiled proudly as he focused his eyes back on me.

"JU LIKE WHAT YOU SEE, CHICA?" Surprisingly, Roberto's dick was a nice size. It wasn't as big as Malice's dick, but it was definitely putting in some work. The chick that he was fucking didn't even care to stop moaning as he kept sliding in and out of her. Her eyes started rolling back and her eyes shut tightly like she was in heaven.

"IF MY HERMANO doesn't do it like this..."

MALICE GRABBED me by the hand and slammed the door shut behind us. I couldn't contain my laughter anymore. I grabbed my knees and roared loud, hearing my giggles bounce off the walls, Malice mumbled.

"WAIT until I tell Killa and Big B this shit." He had turned a shade of red like he couldn't believe what we just walked in and saw.

· · ·

WE MADE it to his room, and I stripped out of my clothes. When I turned to look at Malice, he was sitting on the edge of his bed looking confused.

"Is that nigga gay still or does this make him straight." He looked up at me and my eyes fell down to his flaccid dick. Although it was soft as hell it still laid long and thick against his thigh.

I SAID nothing as I walked up to him and stood between his legs. I didn't give a damn about what Roberto had going on. All I wanted was for Malice to fuck me or I was going to fuck him. Seeing that he was still confused by what he saw I picked my left leg up and placed it on the bed as I grabbed my nipples and pinched them, rubbing them between my fingers. I reached down between my sticky thighs and ran my fingers down my slippery slit. Hissing softly, I grabbed the back of Malice head and pushed his head between my thighs.

HIS TONGUE automatically went to work, he was eating me so damn good that I couldn't stand still. I whimpered softly and felt myself on the verge of tears. His thick tongue and the way he applied heavy ass pressure. I've never felt so good before in my life.

MALICE ATE my pussy like he was in love with it. No timid shit at all. Feeling his hands all over me, the way he caressed my ass. Capturing my clit softly between his teeth then nibbling, he sucked the pain away then licked my clit until it swelled up with anticipation.

RIGHT WHEN I was about to cum, he kissed up my stomach then flicked his tongue in and out of my belly button. Leaning back on his elbows, with his dick sticking right up. I straddled him effortlessly and got the dick that I had been craving and waiting for.

INFERNO

"*H*ow many times, she gon' call?" Killa chuckled as I stared down at my phone then placed it face down on the patio chaise. I looked out towards the beach and stared at Sovereign and Roberto chasing each other on the sand. I had all kinds of thoughts running through my mind and couldn't stop them even if I tried.

"I never seen you like this homie." Killa stared at me in disbelief.

"Like what?" I picked my phone up and just stared at it as it continued to ring for the hundredth time. Kenya had become relentless after these past couple of days. She sent long paragraph text messages and emails. She starts calling for little shit, it was evident that she had lost her fucking mind. When I made it back to the states, I was going to have to sit down and make things clearer to her.

"In love, nigga. Look how you staring at her. We all see it, it's surprising as fuck but it's a good look on you." I raised my brow to that and didn't say anything. I didn't think about love. With Sovereign, I knew it had to be something stronger than just liking her. She had me sitting in meetings that didn't

81

have shit to do with the syndicate nor the Ruiz cartel. I sat beside her because I wanted to be there for her after she opened up and told me everything there was that I needed to know about her.

I slept with Mi'elle a couple of times after Sovereign, and I had that talk just to see if what I was feeling for Sovereign was real. Reality hit me when I was buried deep inside of Mi'elle. I kept picturing Sovereign and the way she felt and realized that I was wasting my time even fucking on someone else.

The only problem was, I didn't know if I was ready for something so fucking serious. Sovereign had experienced heartbreak multiple times, each heartbreak she created a protective border around her heart. I wanted to be something different for her. I wanted to show her that I could make her happy. She deserved that shit, plus when she was happy it made her beauty stick out even more.

"I've never been in love before Kill, I don't even know what that shit is." I stated honestly, I sat up in the lounge chair when I saw Roberto pick Sovereign up. He had a handful of ass captured in his hands as he ran toward the waves. Sovereign looked picture-perfect with her head back, mouth open laughing loudly.

"In love looks like this nigga. You looking like you ready to fuck Roberto ass up. Nigga is gay, you ain't got to worry about him and Queen." Killa chuckled but my face remained stone.

"I do, I caught that nigga fucking a pretty ass bitch yesterday." This time Big B sat up and looked at me like I had two heads.

"What do you mean?" Big B deep-ass voice rumbled.

"I caught the nigga knee-deep in some pussy. Wasn't a tranny either, real pussy my nigga."

"So the nigga just act feminine to get pussy?" Killa looked like he was actually thinking about the shit which made me shake my damn head.

"I don't know man. I just know he was fucking a bad bitch."

"So he ain't gay?" Big B asked, still looking shocked.

"Nigga, I asked Sovereign the same shit, she shut me up by fucking the shit out of me. Late last night, I came to my own conclusions. Roberto claims he delivered and all that shit from fucking on niggas. In my mind though, once a nigga fuck a nigga, ain't no coming back from that." I shrugged.

"Yea you're right, but for a bitch is different." Killa sounded sure of himself, but I shook my head no, as I declined another call from Kenya.

"No, it's the same for bitches who fuck on bitches. I feel like once you stepped into that lane, you gon' always have those tendencies even if you try to go back straight."

"I gotta disagree with that, plenty of bitches that I've fucked on stop being gay. They even married a nigga!" Killa tried to back up what he was saying, he was wasting his time though because once I came down to a conclusion about some shit, I stuck to it.

"I bet them same bitches still look at other bitches and think the same way us niggas think."

"Hell, yea they do." Big B sat back and took the blunt from behind his ear.

"Since when you start talking so much, nigga." Killa looked over at Big B, who offered him a lazy smile.

"I talk all the time I just don't run my mouth like you all the time." That was true, out of all three of us, Killa talked the most, half the time what he talked about was bullshit.

I decided to go ahead and answer the phone because Kenya was really starting to piss me the fuck off.

"Yea," I answered listening to her heavy breathing. I looked out towards the water and stood up. I was ready to snatch Sovereign ass up. Her body was drenched with water, from here I could tell that her nipples were hard as fuck. Sovereign jumped up on Roberto's back and all I could think about was her fat ass pussy pressed up on this nigga back.

Brother or not, I didn't want the nigga knowing what my wife pussy felt like.

"Inferno? Did you hear me?" Kenya voice sounded pathetic as hell.

"Yea, I hear you... You were saying something went wrong with my business?"

"Umm, no... I just miss you, Inferno. Why won't you talk to me? I just want to know what I did wrong and how can I fix it." I took the phone away from my ear and just stared at it. I wasn't used to Kenya being so needy. In the beginning, she made it seem like she was fine with what it was we were doing. Now it seemed like a woman that I had been doing wrong.

How can I do her wrong when I had always been upfront with her since the first time, I gave her this dick.

"Kenya, look... I think to save your feelings, your job and more importantly your life. We should cut off whatever you think we have in your mind."

"Why? Because of that bitch?" She sniveled hard into the phone and made a hiccup noise.

"No, Kenya. I'm cutting this off because I no longer want to fuck you." I looked off towards the water and my eyes landed on Sovereign. She had her hands on her knees throwing her ass in a circle. Water was dripping off her brown skin, she looked like she was having fun with Roberto as he hyped her up. "I don't know Kenya." I paused and she remained quiet.

I couldn't believe that I was about to actually say this shit. I felt it and never was the type to run from how I was feeling. I was infatuated with Sovereign like I was infatuated with starting and watching fires burn. Sovereign had me stuck and the good part about it all was that she really belonged to me. She was my wife, and I realized that watching her laugh and just be herself showed me that no matter how powerful you were, you still remained a human.

I constantly remained wrapped in my syndicate and counting time as money I didn't do anything to feel normal. I didn't laugh much, didn't indulge in fun shit like Sovereign was doing now. I considered fucking Kenya or Mi'elle as a hobby. I thought sitting with Killa and Big B talking about a bunch of nothing was considered my down and free time.

"I only want to fuck my wife, Kenya. I'll be in touch with you soon so we can sort out your next steps in the syndicate." I hung up in her face and tossed my phone onto the chaise.

I took off my shoes and my shirt and walked off toward the beach. The closer I got to Sovereign the harder my heart started to beat. Was I falling in love or just in deep infatuation? I didn't know what it was but who was going to stop me? No one. I walked up behind Sovereign and pulled her into me. She smelled like her sweet fragrance mixed with the ocean.

"Roberto fucked my hair up." She held onto my forearms with her cold wrinkly fingers and giggled.

"I see, but I like your hair curly, and your body wet as fuck." My voice deepened. "Don't ever put your pussy on another nigga's back." She turned and bit her lip, smirking at me mischievously.

"You jealous?" she taunted and walked backwards towards the water as I followed her.

"Hell yea, I don't like that shit. Plus, Roberto is fucking

women now. I gotta determine if he wants to fuck my wife."
We both fell out laughing as Roberto switched his damn hips.
I couldn't take his ass serious. He had on some skintight
cheetah swim trunks.

"Sovereign is like my sister. I wouldn't fuck her, but she
does look good." He winked at her.

"Why you didn't tell me you were bi?" I asked my
brother seriously.

"Y'all never ask me my preference. You and Pa, just think
I'm fully gay because I enjoy dressing and being feminine. I
love fucking women more than I do men. Sometimes I have a
boyfriend then at times, I feel like having a sexy woman.
Being with a woman is fun for me because we both get to go
on nail and hair dates." He shimmied his shoulders and then
ran off towards the beach. He did three backflips and started
to swim. Sovereign pulled my hand and took me towards the
ocean.

"I don't really swim like that Sovereign," I warned her as
the water came up to my ankles.

"Let me teach you then, Burna boy." She smiled as she
jumped up into my arms, wrapping her thick legs around me.

I licked and sucked on her neck as the water welcomed us
in. Looking into her hazel-brown eyes had me in a trance. I
had a funny feeling in my gut and tried to change the topic so
I wouldn't ruin the moment.

"You didn't ask me to come with you today to meet with
your Abuela." I wanted to know how that went. Miguella had
been giving Sovereign the run around with telling her the
secret whereabouts of this nigga Melvin. I personally didn't
know this nigga, but I knew he was a problem. I didn't do
problems, I fixed them before they got to be something else.

Finding out his first and last name was easy, and I already

had my people on top of it. Sovereign was now a part of me and any problem of hers was a problem of mine.

"She said she will give me an address by next week. I guess the location that she had on him has been deserted." She looked off for a minute then focused back on me. I can tell she was bothered by it and was ready to just end it all.

"You believe what she telling you?" I needed to see where her mind was. I didn't want to overstep what she wanted to do concerning her family but if it was left up to me, their skeletons would be souvenirs in Hades by now.

"Of course, I don't, I just hope by next week she gives me what I want. I'm ready to move on to the next phase of all of this." I slid my hands up her chest to her shoulders and grabbed her chin and pulled her close. Gently kissing her soft lips, I felt everything getting intense between us as her eyes fluttered, she struggled with keeping them open.

"I want us to move as a team, I respect everything there is that you got going on. I just want you to remember that I'm a grown-ass man and won't stand in the shadows of my wife while she tries to figure things out." I reminded her how things were supposed to go. I never imagined myself trying a relationship but that didn't mean that I didn't know how one was supposed to go.

I didn't like the way my father did my mom, but I also wished she would give him a second chance. My father realized so much after my mom left him. My parent's relationship was the main reason why I chose to keep things real with females from jump especially if I didn't see myself being with them.

With Sovereign though, I wanted to try this shit for real. In my mind we were good for each other, we could balance each other out. Sovereign and I could be a real powerhouse couple, we complimented each other even though we had some differences.

Even now as we stood in the cold water in the public's eye, it felt like it was just us together. She didn't have on any make up just lip gloss, I was staring at the raw beautiful Sovereign.

"Why you looking at me like that?" She blushed as I pushed some of her hair behind her ear and grabbed each side of her face. I looked her deep in the eyes and just continued to look into her face before I spoke straight from the heart.

"Everything about you is just beautiful as fuck Sove. I mean you sexy from the soles of your feet to them wild-ass baby hairs that's throwing up gang signs right now. You built different baby, that shit turn a nigga on. Yesterday when we caught Roberto fucking, you pulled your gun just like I pulled mine and I know without a doubt you are willing to ride for me, so, let me ride for you." She blushed hard; her brown skin turned rosy.

She tried to look away from me, but I held her face tighter.

"I don't know what this is, Malice. I been moving alone for a while now, as you can see the closest people to me, ends up hurting me the worse. I tried this whole being down for a nigga and it got me looking for him right now trying to end him for good." Her eyes glossed up and she stopped talking when she realized that her words were starting to chop up.

She stilled as she sucked in a hard breath, glancing over my shoulder she watched Roberto walk away from us to give us more privacy.

"I can't make you trust me, but I can show you that shit. I never had my heart broken but I'm not scared to try some new shit with you. I know that you got to believe in your future more than your past. I also know that you break your own heart by making somebody more important to you than you are to them. Never play with yourself like that again baby, especially when there are signs along the way." I grabbed her hand and led her out of the water.

"Until you become certain with what you want to make out of us, I still want us to move as one when it comes to this bitch ass nigga Melvin and your Abuela and whoever else. I don't want you feeling like you got to face any of this shit alone. Rather we started off as business are not, you are a Ruiz, my wife and I'm ready to move just like a husband should behind this."

I slapped and grabbed a hand full of ass and loved the way it felt like jello in my hands. My dick stiffened as I watched her ass move to its own beat in front of me. I wanted her pussy and inner thighs drenched by the time we showered and got in bed. I was getting used to this woman being in my bed and in my home. The unique smell she gave my room and the feeling she gave me in general was addicting as hell.

"You so damn nasty and I like that shit. I hope you mean what you say Malice. I hope this is something you really want. I want to take shit slow, but I meant what I said when I told you that the dick belongs to me. Don't play dangerous and let it slip into another bitch, cause that could be deadly for the both of you." She winked and put a little more umph and each step she took.

Little did Sovereign know; I loved all that hot shit she talked. That shit drove a nigga crazy when she said that the dick belonged to her. I just hope she knew how crazy a nigga would act if she put that pussy on another nigga.

SOULFUL HURTZ

I hate I came to school dripped the fuck out. I didn't have time to drive to my house and switch my clothing around. I only really came to see Jocelyn; I had been missing her ass like crazy and needed to lay eyes on her even if it was for a couple of seconds. I went through each class period collecting homework and listening to my teachers preach to me about missing school and assignments.

After stuffing my backpack with lots of homework and assignments that I had missed out on. I walked out of my last class feeling a little better. I wasn't too far behind with work, and I also was planning on bringing my mom home for just a couple of hours then putting her back in the hotel that I was funding.

When Luv broke down, I spent weeks combing Watts trying to locate my mom. It wasn't that hard finding her because she was at a new crack spot that was popping with new come up boys that got their hands on some drugs from the African niggas that called themselves trying to make a name for themselves. I already put Sovereign up on game about the new niggas trying to move big work in the urban communities.

That was a no go and sooner or later that would be shut down. That was one of the big reasons that I fucked with Sovereign heavy. She didn't push heavy drugs in the black communities. She dished that shit out to rich neighborhoods that could actually afford the shit. When I found my mom, I placed her in a hotel and told her the date and time that I would be by to pick her up from the hotel.

I told her that I expected her to be sober before I brought her to my place to see the girls. Luv behavior hadn't gotten any better, but I was hoping that we could reason a little. Maybe if she got to see Antionette more that could possibly help with her behavioral issues.

I caught the back of Jocelyn and watched her walk through the back exit. All day at school she had been avoiding me and I knew it was because she was angry with me for curving her. She didn't understand that I did that shit for her own good. Picking up my footsteps, I followed right behind her. My car was parked the front of the school inside the parking lot. Jocelyn switched her ass fast as she talked and walked with her homegirls like she didn't see me trying to catch up with her.

It was crazy that she was even conversing with them broads when two of them passed me notes during class offering to fuck me. I wasn't dusty anymore and now these birds were trying to be down to see what all I could offer them.

"Jocelyn!" I called her name tired of following behind her. She turned around slowly and looked at me with an atti- tude. Placing her hand on her small curvy hip, she poked her lip out and stood in the same spot close to the curb. The closer I got the more uncomfortable she seemed to be. She looked nervous as hell, and I didn't understand why.

Choosing to not say anything to her, I pulled her close and hugged her tight. I enjoyed the soft scent of vanilla invading my nose.

"I missed you, Jocelyn." That was the truth, it wasn't a day that went by that I didn't find myself thinking about her and this pretty ass face. I can see her eyes glossing up like I put her through so much turmoil. She looked around at the people near us then pushed her glasses up to the bridge of her nose.

"Soulful, I have a man now." That shit almost knocked me down, but I couldn't be mad at her. Although I liked Jocelyn a lot, I was still laying pipe to a couple of females when I found the time to.

"What that got to do with me? You give him your virginity?" I frowned and when she got quiet, I was ready to turn up on her. Sensing my anger, she quickly shook her head no, and I calmed down a bit. I dug in my back pocket and handed her my iPhone. Without saying too many words she punched her number in then handed me my phone back. I was happy that I now had a number on her. Sometimes I just wanted to hear her voice, I had a lot going on right now and didn't want Jocelyn mixed up with my problems.

"You need a ride home?" I didn't plan on going that way but for Jocelyn, I would. Since I was making lots of money now, I tried to stay far away from the hood. If it didn't have anything to do with finding my momma, then I figured I didn't have any business over that way.

I wasn't scared of niggas, but I also knew that I wasn't untouchable. I bled like the rest of these niggas and didn't want to chance having to lay another nigga down. I noticed a big body Benz pulling up to the curb with tinted windows and music blasting. Jocelyn body language changed to, so I took a couple steps away from her.

"It was good seeing you, Soulful. Call me whenever you get the time." She touched my arm and then quickly walked away. Watching her get into a car with another nigga and knowing that she was giving him time and attention didn't sit to well with me. I knew that I was that nigga that could treat Jocelyn right and not just use her to get what I wanted since she looked so fucking good.

All the way to my car, I thought about calling Jocelyn and taking her ass home with me. For now, I had shit to do and that was see about my stubborn ass momma.

* * *

I STOOD in front of my mom hotel door and dreaded picking up my fist to knock. I hope she listened to what I told her ass and sobered up. There was no way, I was bringing her to my house high off drugs. Finally knocking on the door, I got irritated with how long she took to open it.

She looked frailer like she lost even more weight. I could tell she was having withdrawals because she was shaking like the weather was zero degrees. Her long brittle hair was slicked back into a ponytail, and she sported some sweatpants and a graphic Tupac shirt.

"Hey, Soulful. Just come in for a while, I got to finish packing my bag." I nodded and remained quiet. Walking into her room, my stomach instantly turned. It smelled like ass and cigarettes mixed with the smell of beer. The room didn't look cluttered or a mess so I took a seat in the loveseat that sat in the corner next to the window and AC vent.

"I can't wait to see my girls. I miss them and you, so much." She picked up her backpack from the floor and looked over at me with sad eyes. I wanted to talk but couldn't. I was still picturing her at that park with Passion, out of it and being raped in front of my little sister. Every time I thought about that shit, I found myself getting emotional. I just didn't understand why my momma couldn't get right for us.

She didn't say anything when she noticed that I wasn't offering her much conversation. She looked nervous and like she wanted to say more. When she was done gathering her things she turned back around and looked at me.

"You know why you caught me like that Soulful?" She shivered like she was cold and scratched at her small arms. "I was willing for them niggas to run a train on me. I would never pimp my baby out for drugs! I went to that park itching for a hit but when they started talking about the debt I owed and how they were going to do horrible things to my baby, I allowed them to take turns fucking me!" She sobbed as I roughly wiped at my own tears.

It never amazed me how much I allowed this woman to hurt me. I could never stop the love I had for my mother and treat her cold, but I couldn't be weak for her anymore.

"That explanation ain't enough for me, ma." I shook my head and bowed my head.

"I can't keep letting you do this to us! I'm grown now but before being grown I've been carrying us on our backs! That ain't shit to brag about though. I did that shit cause I ain't have a choice and I love the fuck out of my sisters and you! Damn ma…" I took a deep breath. It felt like each breath that I took was painful. Sharp pains hit my chest; the tears kept falling but this time faster. "I had and have so many fuckin issues that you never saw and tried to talk about it with me." I cleared my throat and wiped my tears.

"I'm a new person ma, the only relationship you can try

to fix is the ones you have with Luv and Passion. They love the fuck out of you, and I don't knock them for it because I love you a lot too. That shit will never change, but I'm done allowing you to hurt me. Only reason I'm here right now is for the sake of my siblings." I stood and went to the door to wait out in the car for her.

One day, I knew I would have to forgive my momma but right now I just couldn't. I thought back to Jocelyn and decided that I was willing to make her mine again. I didn't like the idea of her being with another nigga. Once I sorted some shit out and got things more solid on my end I was coming for my girl and claiming her as mine.

SOVEREIGN

I sat in the backseat of Bundy's Jaguar with a blunt dangling from my lips. Ignoring Malice call had me feeling like I was up to some shit that I had no business doing. After getting the run around about where Melvin was, my Abuela finally sent me a text with an address and time to find and kill Melvin.

ANXIOUSNESS FILLED me to the core, and I was ready to put this nigga in the dust. I know I did a lot of confiding in Malice and he was proving to me day by day that he was actually here for me. I appreciated that shit to the fullest but at the end of the day. I was a gangsta and could handle my own shit however I saw fit.

I DIDN'T NEED a crew to go on missions with me. Whenever I personally went out to kill a person it meant that it was personal and beyond business. Bundy and I were like thieves in the night, all black with steel-toe boots parked in the back of the woods with no headlights on.

THE HOUSE WAS BEAUTIFUL, it stuck out like a sore thumb, like it was too perfect to be in the area that it was in. Coming from the city of Los Angeles, this area gave peace and quiet with lots of privacy something this nigga Melvin didn't deserve. It was like a lakeside retreat surrounded by tall oak trees and plants. When you looked up into the sky you could see a clear view of the moon and dozens of stars.

WE WERE IN ORLANDO, somewhere I would have never thought this nigga would be.

"I'LL GO in through the back." I scrolled through my text messages stopping at the one from Malice. I smiled and locked my phone; Malice would have to learn exactly who he was married too.

"NO, THE FRONT, QUEEN." I looked up at Bundy and frowned. I didn't like receiving orders from anyone.

"The back door is easier to get into." I shrugged him off, but he was persistent.

"THE FRONT, Queen. You always go through the back when going after someone. Try the front door this time. I just think the front will be better in this case." Bundy turned all the way around and stared at me seriously.

. . .

"I NEVER SAW you nervous Bundy. It's not a good look on you." I rolled the window down a little and flicked the blunt out the window, then rolled it back up. I put on my black leather gloves and pulled my Celine mask down to cover my full face. The only thing that was exposed was my lips. I had my wild curly hair tamed and pulled back into a braid.

"I'M NOT NERVOUS, just cautious. This nigga ain't as dumb as we might think he is. Melvin has been clever enough to not be caught by you after all these years." I cringed at that but couldn't get mad. Everything he was saying was the truth, so I guess I would go through the front this time instead of the back. I secured my AR and stepped out the car feeling queasy as hell.

I FELT dizzy like I stood up too fast, my mouth felt watery, I gathered all the salvia that built up in my mouth and spit it out. That didn't stop the salvia from building up inside of my mouth. Suddenly, Bundy crashed on top of me throwing me down into the bushes.

"STAY DOWN QUEEN, red beams on you coming from the fucking house. I don't know if we are outnumbered but we have a good distance. We gone have to retreat." He talked fast as he held me tight with his body shielding mine. I chuckled as anger flared up inside of me. Did my Abuela set me up? If I made it out of this alive, she was the first person that I was gon' go see about.

. . .

"GET OFF OF ME BUNDY, I don't need you taking a bullet for me." He moved a little but still stayed hovered on top of me as my phone sounded off. My eyes got big at the red beam pointed at the center of Bundy's head.

I ANSWERED the phone and said nothing, my stomach fluttered, and I swallowed down the urge of hurling all over myself.

"STILL THE SAME QUEEN." His voice made laugh a little harder. "Got dayum, I miss that sexy ass laugh too." His deep ass voice chuckled into the line as I squeezed the phone tightly.

"MELVIN." My voice was flat of any emotion. I tried to remain calm, but I was raging on the inside.

"SAY MY NAME BABY." He cooed into the line.

"YOU ARE ON BORROWED TIME." I gritted.

"YEA? I figured that. Tell that big nigga to get off of you before I have my men put a bullet threw his dome." I moved a little and mouthed off to Bundy that it was okay to get off of me.

. . .

"STAND UP, Queen...let me see you. It's been years and you being this close got me ready to nut all over this bitch face." I stood up slowly and dusted myself off as Bundy stood behind me.

"ALL THAT MUTHAFUCKIN' ass. Get on your knees and suck this dick while I talk to the love of my life." I lost it as I listened to a woman sucking him off, I could hear her spitting and gagging as he grunted hard into the phone.

I MOVED AWAY from Bundy and bent over and released everything I had inside of me. This nigga had me sick to my stomach and I couldn't stop throwing up, until I start dry heaving.

"FUCK!" he roared into the phone as I wiped away at my mouth and pulled the Celine mask off my face so I could take in more air. I stood in place nodding my head at Bundy as he asked me if I was okay. On the inside, I felt like shit. I felt like I was coming down with some type of stomach virus.

"YOU WILL MEET with me in a public place, Queen. In about two days. If you come with anyone else or if I see anybody lurking like you are doing now... then things can go bad for your papa and stupid ass sister." He chuckled as I remained quiet, trying to weigh out all of my options.

. . .

"I SUGGEST you go have a sit down with Miguella and get the real scoop from her before you sit down with me, and I finish breaking that weak ass heart of yours. Get the fuck off my property before I peel that niggas head back and send my folks to come to get you. If I had things my way right now, I'd be between those sexy ass thighs fucking the shit out of you relentlessly."

HE HUNG up in my face and I stood there for a couple of seconds. I was boiling with anger as I walked back towards the car. I slid into the backseat and said nothing until my anger bubbled over and I found myself not being able to hold in my laugh of anger.

* * *

I WOKE up sweating and choking from what smelled like a burning fireplace. My body was naked and drenched, the heat smothering me. My body stuck to the silk sheets, and I had already known that Malice kidnapped me once again. His room was pitch black, the only thing that could be seen was the flicker of flames coming from his massive fireplace. My mind automatically went to Bundy. We got on my private jet to Mexico and checked in an all-exclusive hotel.

ALL NIGHT I found myself sick and throwing up with thoughts of being that close to Melvin and failing once again at killing him. Bundy slept in the living room of our suite but constantly ran in and out of the room passing me blunts and ginger ale to get my stomach to settle. I wasn't even surprised waking up inside of Malice home.

. . .

I KNEW after ignoring his calls for the third or fourth time he would come for me. It's like he had a built in GPS on my ass and wouldn't let up if he didn't get what he wanted.

I TOOK a deep breath and licked my dry lips. I automatically became annoyed with how hot he had me in this damn room of his. He was doing this shit on purpose, and it was working because it was so fucking hot in here, that I felt weak like I was close to fainting.

"I HAD to turn the temperature up around this bitch, just so you can see what it's like to play with fucking fire. You keep testing that shit out until it melts you into nothing." His deep ass voice sounded off from the corner of his dark room. I coughed a little then sat up in the bed looking around at nothing. The only thing I could see was the surrounding area of where his fireplace sat.

"I ALMOST SKINNED that nigga Bundy alive tonight. I let the nigga live because he had the decency to call me and tell me where the fuck y'all were... sharing a fucking room. Why he in the same space as you? Seems very intimate, Sovereign."

"IT WAS BUSINESS. Bundy works for me, so rather you like it or not he will assist whenever I see fit." I got out of the bed and stretched.

. . .

"WHILE YOU'RE PREGNANT, with my seed?" His voice deepened and sounded darker. I froze in the same spot as he clapped his hands. The lights came on but not bright, just dim. The perspiration now looked like someone dumped a bucket of water on my body. I could feel the sweat dripping from my chin sliding down between my breasts.

"KENYA MONROE, works for me as well and she does a damn good job. However, I have taken the intimacy that I once given her away on account of you. Do you get what the fuck I am saying to you?" He stood up, I could see fire dancing in his eyes.

HIS GOATEE HAD GROWN out by a couple of inches, he stood up with nothing but silk boxers on. Malice's short curls looked like tight coils and somehow his masculine woodsy aroma filled the space we occupied.

"I GET what you are saying, Malice. This was business." I didn't like how I was feeling right now. I felt sweaty and uncomfortable, the way Malice stared at me was with hunger like he was ready to devour me. That sick feeling erupted in the pits of my stomach, and I felt the urge again to throw up.

"I'M NOT PREGNANT." I reassured him, there was no way. My insides were fucked up from the hood abortion I got years ago. I couldn't conceive there was no point in me even giving it a second thought. The only experience I had with a failed pregnancy was Melvin's baby. I felt sick just like I was feeling now, and the doctor told me it was a chemical pregnancy.

IT WAS A VERY early miscarriage that happened within the first five weeks of pregnancy. The embryo formed and was embedded in the lining of my uterus lining but stopped developing. I went through a painful miscarriage with lots of heavy blood. The doctor said it was from chromosomal problems with the developing baby, but I didn't believe that shit. Something deep inside of me knew that I couldn't carry because of that damn abortion I had. I felt like I was cursed from that point on, so I stopped dreaming about having a fucking kid.

"YOU SAY it's just business like you said about our marriage but even you and I know that it was all a lie. I'm starting to think you like when I'm on edge, Sovereign. And in a very toxic way I like seeing your crazy too. It turns me the fuck on, but this type of crazy is different from you. It's the type of crazy that can very well get a nigga killed." He stepped into my personal space and placed his hands on my curvaceous hips.

"BEING in a hotel with another man other than me while you're carrying my baby is beyond crazy. He doesn't even know how to tend to you properly baby. You got a nigga threatening my pilot to get me to Mexico in a short amount of time just to see about you. Tell me Sovereign, do you really think that this thing between us is still business?" He lowered his head, I backed away. My heart speeding up at just his words alone.

. . .

"YOU'RE SCARED, it's understandable but you have to accept just what this is." I shook my head no, and tried to turn away from him, but he grabbed me tight and pulled me into him. His hands were slipping off of my drenched body as he clung on no matter how wet my entire body was.

"I WANT you bad as fuck, Sovereign. You got to understand the patience I'm trying to have. If it was left up to me, you'd be glued to my side living in my homes wherever I go. I'd slide in you raw every fucking night. This baby growing in you... is just the beginning like it's the beginning of our relationship. I'm crazy about you and I'm rich as fuck baby. That says a whole lot, I don't and won't hold back how the fuck I feel. It's to make things clearer for how crazy I'm willing to get behind you. Don't ever let what happened yesterday happen again, Sove... you understand right?"

I COULD'VE SWORN I seen his left eye twitch. He let me go and went to stand next to the fireplace. He left me standing in the same spot speechless, looking at his well-defined back. No matter how hard I found myself pulling away from Malice. He'd end up saying or doing some shit that sent me lurching forward and falling hard for his ass. A baby? He really believed that I had a baby growing inside of me. I didn't want to disappoint him.

"I CAN'T CONCEIVE, Malice. I had an abortion when I was young, and I think they messed some stuff inside of me up." I cleared my throat. He didn't turn to look at me, he just watched the fire like it was his favorite TV show.

"You don't know that for sure. You forget you told me this already. That was a long time ago. Doesn't mean my semen isn't strong enough to send my son right into your uterus." He put the fire out and went to the window to let air in the room.

"Come shower with me, so you can tell me all about this mission you went on with Bundy." He walked towards his bathroom. I dropped my head momentarily but picked it up and walked right behind him.

After showering and going into detail about everything that had transpired over the last twenty-four hours. I laid on Malice chest and listen to his heartbeat as we talked some more. The feeling was everything. He made me some tea that settled my stomach immediately and I knew he had to bring some of the herbs and spices his house maid provided. My eyes got heavy again and I found myself ready to close my eyes.

"You are going to see Miguella in the morning. I will have a talk with her first. I don't know what games she's playing but it's time to put an end to this cat and mouse shit. You want to kill Melvin, I'll respect that. You won't be meeting him in a public place alone though. So, don't answer none of them unknown calls." He stopped talking like he was thinking. I watched the way his long curly eye lashes tickled the heavy lid of his prominent eyelid.

"YOU GETTING a new phone in the morning too. When we leave Mexico, I'm taking you to the doctor." Butterflies swarmed in my stomach. I never had a man this bold enough to take the initiative. This shit was turning me on and making me feel special as hell.

"YOU STILL THINKING about turning the cartel over to Roberto?" I wanted to know. I imagined my business ending out here in Mexico after being done with Abuela. All money wasn't good money, and I wouldn't be able to sleep well until I avenged my mother properly.

"YEA, I plan on going to see my mom this week. When I come back out here, I plan on talking to Roberto and my dad." My heart flared a little.

"SO, if we both no longer apart of this cartel shit, then where does that leave us? We won't have anything forcing us to keep us married." I couldn't believe how sad I sounded saying this, I couldn't hide the disappointment.

LOOKING UP IN MALICE, magical eyes gave me all the reassurance that I needed in this moment.

. . .

"THAT'S EVEN BETTER, you not going nowhere. You are going to remain my wife. When I go to see my mom, you coming with me." He captured my lips with his.

"I DON'T NEED cartel money and you don't either as long as you are my wife." This time instead of him kissing me again, first I threw my arms around him and pulled him until he was on top of me between my legs. I brought his head down until his thick lips aligned with mine. I kissed him passionately like my life depended on it.

GASPING at the feel of him invading my snug tunnel, I received all of him as he rocked in and out of me.

"YOU PREGNANT WITH MY BABY, this pussy biting differently, baby." He talked directly in my ear as he pulled my double D breast up to his lip and sucked on my tender nipple.

"PUSSY FEEL DIFFERENT, shit gone have me keeping that ass pregnant. We got enough money for a football team." I blushed and moaned hard at his revelation as he kept stroking me with precision. This man was forcing my stubborn ass to be hooked on him.

IF HE GAVE ME A BABY, that would overjoy me, I didn't want to get my hopes up. Malice had me ready to say fuck meeting with Abuela. I wanted to see if a baby was growing inside of me. If it was a baby, then I would let

Malice teach me how to suck his thick long ass dick as a thank you.

I WOKE UP CRANKY, Malice only let me sleep for about four hours before he woke me up. It was seven in the morning, he had oatmeal and toast waiting for me to eat. I chased it down with some kind of tea that he promised would help with feeling sick. My body still felt weak, but I was ready to get today over with. I planned on resting once I made it back to Cali. I was literally tired of flying back and forth every other week just to talk face to face with these old school cartel members that didn't believe in having burner phones or secured lines where you could talk freely.

MY ABUELA WAS one of those people that had to talk face to face. I walked with a slight limp and my kitty purred out in pain from the hurting Malice put on it last night. I was redirected by my Abuela's men that she was inside the sunroom, having her morning soak. I rolled my eyes because she swore that these special baths would help her retain her youthful looks, but she seemed to turn more wrinkled each time I laid eyes on her.

WHEN I WALKED into the sunroom, Malice informed me that he'd have a talk with Abuela when the time was right, he seemed disgusted with talking to her while she soaked in a milk bath surrounded by flowers. He turned right around and busied himself on his phone. I admired all the different flowers that sat in each corner of the sunroom. Even the garden tub that she soaked in was surrounded by different wildflowers. She had petals in the tub. Cucumbers covered her eyes as she held a champagne flute in her hand.

"Mɪ Nɪᴇᴛᴀ." (My granddaughter) "You didn't have a successful mission, I see." She smiled and sat up a little to take a sip of her wine.

"I ᴅɪᴅɴ'ᴛ, and I'm tired of playing games with you. I'm also tired of faking shit as well." Her mouth fell open as I squatted next to the tub, watching her take the cucumbers off of her eyes.

"Yᴏᴜ ᴋɪʟʟᴇᴅ ᴍʏ ᴍᴏᴛʜᴇʀ." My eyes burned as I stood up and stepped away from her.

"Sɪ, I did, and I was and still am, fucking the man that killed her for me, Mi Nieta. I thought you'd never figure it out." She smiled evilly as I laughed a little. Pain hit my chest although I already knew the truth.

"Oᴜʀ ʙᴜsɪɴᴇss, is done. I'm pretty sure we are now considered to be at war." I never blinked my eyes.

"Oʜ ɴᴏ, Mi Nieta. We could never be at war, ju see... I own you, you little classless black bitch." She sat up so fast the milk that she soaked in spilled out from the sides of the tub.

· · ·

"I OWN you so bad that if you tried to walk away from everything that I have set in motion, I will destroy you like I did Sovereignty and that worthless ass son of mine who in fact should be happy and grateful that I kept him alive." She looked so sure of her words that to a weak person it would be chilling. To me it meant nothing because I already knew the truth. She wanted to see me break in front of her, but I would eat glass before I gave her the satisfaction.

"YOU, Mi Nieta, should thank me too. Money and power of this status gets you the world handed to you. Not feelings and love. You went through what you went through as a young teen to build characteristics. A street thug you became instead of turning to me and letting me properly groom you. You would've had a better life if you hadn't run off. Empress would've been better and married off at eighteen instead of fucking your man." She giggled a little then hit me with a gut punch to the stomach with her words alone.

"I NEEDED to see what had you sisters acting so weak for a man. I fucked Melvin too. I only kept him alive this long because he sexes me better than his father."

"YOU'RE DEAD TO ME." I hissed with my lips so tight I could feel each crease.

"SI, and you are alive to me. You will thrive and hate me. There is nothing you can do about it. Now that we have that out the way, you need to leave, I need to enjoy my beauty soak. I will call for you to return in a couple of weeks. We will be celebrating my special day." She smiled wide at me and picked up her cucumbers without a care in the world, placing them back on top of her sagging eyelids she started to hum.

SHE WAS SO confident and at peace that she didn't bother to acknowledge me again. I blew her a kiss because really soon she would be getting sent straight to hell. Underestimating me was like underestimating your life expectancy. I was about to make it my duty to send this bitch and her demons straight to Hades.

I DON'T KNOW why people thought my middle name was pussy. My mother was sweet as fuck but even she stood her ground when it came to Miguella's evil ass. I really hated the fact that my mom had to lose her life to this weird ass bitch. When I thought about the whole situation, I felt myself getting sick all over again.

KENYA MONROE

e all sat in the meeting room anxious to see our boss. I probably felt more anxious than the rest because it has been months since I have even been able to lay eyes on Inferno. I tried my hardest to place my focus on the syndicate and playing my part to make sure everything was going how it should have been. I even started going on dates with Bundy, but we hadn't made it to the sexual part of all of our encounters.

"You show look good as hell today, Kenya Monroe." Killa licked his lips and winked at me. He gave me a knowing look and I rolled my eyes hard at his annoying ass. It was probably obvious that I came dressed to impress. I missed spending time with Inferno. I stopped calling him to show him that I didn't need or want him. I even tried to give most of my time to Bundy. Bundy was actually a sweetheart and I liked him. He just wasn't Inferno and that was the only thing I couldn't push myself to get over.

The problem was when I was with Bundy, I pushed Inferno out of my mind. When I wasn't talking to Bundy and working by myself or at home looking at Inferno side of the closet watching his clothes collect dust. I laid in bed and cried myself to sleep. It wasn't to the point of me trying to harm myself, but it was close. I was going through a terrible heart break and nothing that I was trying to do with myself was helping me get over this man.

It was a dull and piercing ache in the center of my chest. It was depleting me; the heart break was so chronic that I couldn't even think straight. It felt like I had a permanent migraine that wouldn't go away with pills or any other substance. Today I put pounds of make up on my face just to cover my baggy eyes. I didn't have the urge to eat and only slept when my body gave in to needing some form of rest.

I was so disgusted with myself that I vowed to let Inferno go. Nobody should feel this way and feel as though it was normal. I told myself every single day to let this man go but my heart just couldn't agree with my brain. I felt myself losing my mind trying to get myself to let go was the hardest part.

I woke up this morning and put on my most expensive designer clothes, skintight showing off the small curves that I was starting to lose from starving myself to death.

Big B opened the glass door and Killa started to laugh lowly. Big B always had a bad fashion sense. He was a big burly man that was tall and big as hell. He loved wearing clothes that were too tight and he never matched to save his life.

"Bro what the fuck do you be putting on? How do you even get pussy." Killa clowned because he was just the ignorant prick that couldn't control himself. Big B flicked him off, his dark black eyes swept the room daring someone to find what Killa said to be funny.

When his eyes fell on me, he offered a sympathetic look and pushed the door back wider for the man of the hour to enter. I held my breath and fixed my posture as I waited impatiently to see his face. Seconds felt like minutes until he appeared wearing all red. He looked relaxed and laid back. Usually, Inferno always looked like he had a million things on his mind. I was begging with my eyes for him to notice me but his blue, greenish eyes never landed on me.

He pulled out his chair at the end of the table and pulled his phone from his back pocket before sitting down.

"Everybody in this room has been doing a wonderful job. I have no complaints and I don't see the need for any of you to give me an update in this last-minute meeting. Killa and Big B will step up more and be on top of things. I'll be on my honeymoon for a couple of months." He chuckled then finally he looked at me for a couple of seconds. His eyes stayed planted on me and it was at the wrong time. My heart was shattering and it felt like he could hear it breaking.

"Everyone in this room is considered a boss. You all bring something to the table in this underground syndicate. From politics to new franchises. Protection and execution, guns, power and respect. Your families for generations to come will eat well and be established and even their grandchildren. We never played checkers, always chess and for that reason along everyone will receive a bonus and unfortunately some will receive severance pay." My mouth fell slightly open, severance pay? That had to be directed towards me. I shifted uncomfortably as I shook his words off and lowered my eyes away from his orbs.

"Please don't let a healthy severance pay make you turn and become mouthy in the wrong ways. One of my rules about fire is..." he waited for the entire room to say his famous rule together and they roared that shit with pride as I mumbled it.

"You play with fire; you get burned to death by that shit."

My stomach flipped, I licked my lips and sat back in the chair. I tuned out of the rest of the meeting until I heard my name being called by Inferno. I blinked twice and looked over at him holding a yellow envelope. Underneath the yellow envelope was a small square box with a bow on top. He dismissed everyone except me then stood tall and slowly made his way to my side of the table.

He sat the items down in front of me then leaned until he was halfway sitting on the table next to me.

"Kenya Monroe, you have been good to the syndicate and because of that, you will be set for life." He started to give me what seemed to be a farewell speech. I could no longer hold back my emotions as my lips trembled and fear rose high inside of me.

"Inferno, please... don't do this to me, to us!" I choked over my words and stumbled to my feet, so I could face him and humiliate myself for the last damn time.

"I can continue to be good, I won't bother you. I don't expect anything else from you. I have even tried to move on and date someone else." His hot fingers wiped at my tears; he squeezed my chin lightly as he shook his head slowly.

"In that first envelope is a check, Kenya. A check for five million dollars. There's also a NDA that you signed years ago with my signature now added. I understand you are hurt; I also know that sometimes hurt people try to hurt people. I just hope you understand that I'm not the nigga to try to hurt. Your illegal and legal dealings stretch as long as my dick, Kenya." I glanced down at the long dick print that was resting against his thigh.

Both of my lips were trembling uncontrollably and my whole world started to spin.

"Inferno." I pleaded in my small voice.

"She's having my baby Kenya... I'm falling in love with

her Ma." Everything stood still, the time, my feelings, my heart stopped beating as I looked at him with swollen puffy eyes.

"I got love for you Kenya, I'm not as cold hearted as I appear. You a good woman, I just can't keep you around me. I can go on with business and not feel a thing towards you, I just don't want to cut you that deep. You no longer act like the old Kenya Monroe. You act like you deranged, and in love with me. Everybody sees it, and... Kenya, get up." He demanded, but I couldn't. I felt weak and low, all I could think to do was drop down to my knees in front of him. There was no other man like Inferno, why couldn't he just see how badly in love I was with him. Why couldn't he understand how hard I could continue going for this syndicate on behalf of him and the love I had embedded inside of me for only him.

I don't think I even loved my own parents this deeply.

"I care for you Kenya." He picked me up off the floor and held my hands in his. I shivered and shook like it was below zero degrees. "I want to help you Kenya, this behavior isn't normal. You almost got yourself killed popping up at my mom's house."

"Inferno, you're going to kill me, baby. I can't... I just won't... live... without you." I hiccuped hard and choked on my own tears. I probably looked disgusting to him, make up smeared, snot running out my nose. This should make him care and love me more. He should see how bad of a wreck I truly was without him.

"You have no choice, Kenya." That voice pierced through my soul. It belonged to the fat bitch that took my man away. She stood with no makeup and a glow that covered her entire body. I looked back at Inferno and the way he looked at her sickened me to my core. My eyes zeroed in on her stomach and it didn't look like she was pregnant.

"Let her go Inferno. Get your hands off of her and finish up what you have to say." Anger bloomed inside of me, and I envisioned myself stomping the life out of her but I was too scared to even try something of the sort.

"Kenya?" My mouth went dry as Bundy stepped inside the meeting room with a look of concern.

"Kenya this ain't you baby girl." He made his way close to me as I backed up until I was up against Inferno like he was my protector.

"THIS IS ME BUNDY!" I shook as Inferno placed his hands on my shoulder to calm me.

"No, it's not Ma, had I known how small this world was... I would've..." his words trailed off as two men dressed in white entered the room. One had a wheelchair and the other had restraints. I looked around at everyone confused trying to figure out just what was going on. Inferno turned me around until I was facing him, the smell of his breath was intoxicating. I wanted to pull him close and kiss him and stay in his arms forever.

"I care for you Kenya; you got a good heart. I want to help you, so these men here are good friends of mine. They are going to take you to a facility for like six months depending on your behavior and obsession for me. You will be out in Houston, Texas. Your parents are outside, and I have explained enough for them to understand. All your things are packed and ready. You have to go Kenya willingly or unwillingly. I can't trust you by yourself." I lost it.

"I WILL KILL MYSELF INFERNO! IM NOT LEAVING YOU!" I screamed until my head throbbed. I held on tight to him until I felt his shirt rip in my hands. I looked back at Queen who had a pathetic look on her face. I tried to charge her because that bitch didn't know how bad she fucked Inferno and I relationship up. Inferno held his grip tight on me as I grabbed onto his forearm and begged him.

"I'll die Inferno, please don't do this!"

"I have to, and you won't die, that's why I'm getting you help." He nodded at the men as they stepped close to me. I bucked in Inferno's arms and that's when I saw him open the box that had a bow on top. He pulled a long needle out and plunged it into my neck. I grabbed at my neck feeling the sting. A weird sensation took over me and my body became paralyzed. I couldn't move or talk but I could see everybody moving in slow motion.

I could feel my heart beating in my ears and the broken-hearted tunes it played. This was it; I no longer would have Inferno in my life and just maybe it was all for the better.

INFERNO

I felt bad and that meant a lot, it was very rare that I let a situation get to me. Seeing Kenya act out like that made me feel like I made the right decision. It also made me want to treat Sovereign better. No matter how clear I made things to Mi'elle and Kenya and no matter how good Kenya hid how she truly felt it finally spilled over. I hated that I was able to have that type of effect on a woman.

I KNEW she had gone too far when my mom called and told me that she had been by looking for me. My moms cursed me out really good and told me that I was becoming just like my father when it came to women. That was far from the truth because unlike my pops I kept shit a thousand with any female I dealt with. I always made it clear that I would treat them good, but it wouldn't be anything more than sex and conversations here and there. I always considered myself a busy ass businessman and that was true. Deep down I used to feel like I didn't have time to even consider being with someone.

. . .

THEN SOVEREIGN CAME along changing that shit. Sovereign made the saying "making time for who you truly wanted" true. Because I constantly moved my business around in order to chase behind her. I sat in my office watching my nerd squad work hard at changing codes since Kenya was out. I no longer wanted her to know passwords and codes to anything leading to the syndicate.

AFTER GOING to Kenya's home while she was away, I realized how sick she truly was. I thought about killing her to have her permanently removed from my life so she later wouldn't be a problem, but I figure I'd do shit a little differently and get her some mental help. Kenya had dirty boxers of mine underneath the floor bed of her closet. She even managed to cut out a piece of my hair and had it in a box next to what looked like a fucking voodoo doll. On top of all my personal items that Kenya managed to take from me was a card to some witch doctor that was located in New Orleans.

KENYA PLANNED on putting some type of voodoo on a nigga and that shit just wasn't sitting to well with me. I hope she used these six months to get over me and really let go or I else I was going to have to force her to let go and that was through death.

I HAD MORE important shit to tend to, like getting my wife's twisted ass family under one roof and letting her decide who she was going to kill. Her birthday, which she didn't like to acknowledge, was in three weeks and I had a gift that she would forever thank me for.

I STAYED in my office for another two hours and paid my nerd squad extra and tipped them well before I left out with Big B right next to me for our next destination. I already was preparing to face the music with my momma. I wanted her to get on my case hard because tomorrow I planned on letting her meet Sovereign and needed her to be on good behavior.

INFERNO

J arrived outside of my mom's house and a light
drizzle had started. Los Angeles weather was so
bi-polar that you sometimes didn't know what to expect. It
was fifty degrees with high winds in the month of September.
I pulled my phone out and shot my mom a text then
proceeded up the driveway with Big B munching on a pack of
skittles.

I liked having Big B with me because he didn't say much
but caught on to a lot of shit.

"You know they saying that shit causes cancer." I warned
Big B about his skittle intake. Every time I turned around the
nigga had a fresh pack in his hands.

"I know but then again, a lot of shit we eat causes cancer
these days." He shook some in his hands like dice then threw
them back and offered me a big shrug. I chuckled and looked
down at my phone. I saw the three dots appear from my mom
which was unusual. By now she would have already opened
the damn door. She knew like I knew that I didn't like
standing out on the porch. To respect her privacy, I didn't go
barging in her home although I had a key. A couple of minutes

later the bubbles disappeared from our text thread and I heard her heavy footsteps coming towards the front door.

She opened the door smelling like lavender, she gave me an awkward facial expression and stepped to the side to let me and Big B in. I took it as her just being upset with me. Big B and I quietly stepped out of our shoes and socks, something my mom demanded whenever you entered her home. She had a basket next to the front door with fresh pairs of socks for us to put on.

I chuckled at Big B big bulky ass leaning up against the wall for support breathing all hard trying to get on his first pair of socks. When I was done my mom opened her arms and brought me in for a tight hug. Something I always looked forward to whenever I saw her since it wasn't much.

"I missed you Ma." I was way taller than her so when I saw her struggling on her tippy toes, I bent down a little more. Kissing my forehead and grabbing each side of my face with her warm hands I smiled at her.

"Boy, you really got to work on that smile. Y'all have a seat while I go get you some beers." She walked up to Big B and hugged him tightly.

"Where is loud mouth at?" she was referring to Killa obnoxious ass. Something seemed a little off about my mom. I could've sworn I smelled a whiff of cologne, but I shook that suspicion off when I remembered how Big B loved to put on too much cologne whenever he left the house. My mom seemed extra perky, and her chocolate skin was glowing like she was well-rested or some shit.

Something inside of me was telling me to walk around her house and check to see if she had a nigga up in this bitch. My mom was grown and as much as I hated the thought of her with some nigga other than my dad, I had to respect her.

"I don't know my nigga... it seems like moms just got laid." Big B mumbled.

"Fuck you say?" I heard him but wanted to be sure, watching him laugh and munch on them fucking skittles had me tapping my foot hard as my jaw clenched.

"Watch that shit man." Big B offered a taunting look as my mom walked back in the room with beers in her hand. Killa was starting to rub off on Big B cause that was some shit that ignorant nigga Killa would have said. I pulled out my phone and texted Sovereign to see what she was up to. Having a woman that was a boss herself was some hard shit to adapt to. As long as she made time for me like I did for her, I saw no problem with what she was doing.

Further into her pregnancy, I wanted her to rest and focus more on skin care. She gave me a facial a couple of days ago and I was surprised at how magical her hands were. Sovereign was gifted, if she didn't have it so hard coming up, she would have thrived in the field she wanted to thrive in. Now I saw that she was split between wanting to be a Queenpin and still owning and working at her clinic in her free time to clear her mind. We were still adapting to even being a married couple, so I didn't want to come in and start making demands, forcing her to change something she was used to.

Fucking with me, she really ain't have to do shit but look pretty. I just enjoyed watching a woman work as hard as me and love doing it other than sitting at home all day bored coming up with shit to argue about. It was another heavy reason why I didn't want a relationship.

"So, what do I have to do to get my only son to start coming by more?" My mom was beyond beautiful, her smooth chocolate skin was flawless. She was tiny, short and very petite. Her face looked angelic despite her moving up in age.

"I promise to do better, things have been changing. Like I mentioned a couple months back... I met someone." I cleared my throat. My mom was the only person that could make me feel like that little boy that did some bad shit and was bound to get a whooping. I stayed doing some shit growing up. Especially starting fires in our backyard, burning shit up bringing down our property value.

"I hope this someone isn't that girl that came by my home." She snickered sarcastically. "Cause if it is, I'm telling you now, I don't approve."

"I had business a while back with the cartel. Pops had a hit put out on him and I had to assist with his cartel building stronger alliances." I started to explain, as my mom stiffened at the mention of my father. She sat up and crossed her right leg over the left. Raising her eyebrows, she looked at me confused before speaking.

"Your father was shot up and you didn't mention this to me?" She looked like she was bothered and concerned which surprised the hell out of me. I felt a little at ease getting ready to tell her the next part.

"Yea, but we handled all of that. Like I was saying I had to make a business move on behalf of the cartel." I paused to gauge her reaction.

"What was this so-called business move? Your father had no business involving you when he has a mini fucking army of men that works and get a paid good. In fact, did your Pa tell you that he's like the fucking governor of Mexico! Only illegally!" I got a little uncomfortable with how she was now sitting at the edge of the couch like she was ready to stand to her feet. Even Big B felt it all because he pulled out his phone and started pushing buttons. Fake stretching out his limbs, he stood to his feet and placed his phone to his ear. He pointed towards the door and headed in that direction. Any other time this nigga stayed glued to my side, now he was copping out. Straight fuckin comical.

"I understand and know that momma, but I had to do what I had to do." I looked down at my phone, anxious to see what Sovereign had texted back to say. I was now in the hot seat with my mom, so I opted out of even unlocking my phone in front of her.

"What is it that you had to do Malice Ashonti Ruiz!" Her eyes went into tiny slits as I swallowed down and went in for the kill.

"I had to get married, in order to bring three powerful cartels into a new golden triangle." I unlocked my phone and quickly locked it back while jumping backward as my mom leaped to her feet like fire ignited under her.

"You what!!!!!"

"Ma... I really love this girl though." In the middle of pleading my case, I realized that I just confessed my love for the first time for Sovereign. Hell, any woman... I never found myself falling in love with anyone. My heart started to beat differently at my admission. At this very moment, all I wanted to do was be in the presence of my wife.

"Ruiz!!!!!" She screamed as my brows went up. She only called my father by his last name, and I just knew like hell he wasn't here. Seconds later my suspicions were answered. My father walked slowly into the living room wearing nothing but silk boxers. I frowned at the sight of him, he looked like he was comfortable and had been laid up in here for a while. That was his cologne that I smelled.

"Si, bebe?" He ran his fingers through his wild curls and had the nerves to give me an accusing look. I stood to my feet not really feeling this shit anymore. These two had been keeping secrets and my mom had the nerves to come down hard on me.

"Hold up." I took a couple steps back just as my father came to stand next to my mom.

"Y'all two been fucking this whole time?" I asked in disbelief, shaking my head.

"Now Malice, we were going to tell you when the time was right." I shook my head no at her and chuckled in disbelief.

"Nah, you sitting up telling me... I'm just like pops when he got too many wives to count. When I sit up and constantly be honest with these hoes."

"Watch your tone hermano." My father interjected but I was past all the bullshit.

"He's in the process of divorce, I will be his only wife." My mother tried to defend herself, but I just couldn't believe these two. I mean, I always wanted them to be together but the way my mom carried on about my dad over the years I would have never thought they stood a chance at another relationship.

"I don't even care, whatever y'all do is y'all business. Since you here, I might as well save myself a trip and wasting fuel on my jet to tell you that I'm no longer rocking with the cartel shit. Sovereign is pregnant and she cutting ties with Miguella. I don't see neither one of us traveling back and forth to Mexico. You need to talk to Roberto; he is smart as hell and wants more of your attention. He would love to step into your shoes. My focus is here and my syndicate."

I turned towards the door to leave these two alone. I wasn't upset they just caught me by surprise. A nigga like me didn't do too well with surprises. Especially surprises like this, I hated to see the worried look on my mom's face so to make things good before I left. I walked up to her and gave her a hug making sure to plant a kiss on her forehead.

"We should have told you son. I just wanted the divorces finalized before we told you about us reuniting." She looked over to my father and offered me a sad smile.

"You good, I just want y'all both happy and to be happy for me. I really feel like I met my soulmate with Sovereign. I want her to meet you but wanted to tell you about our situation first." A look of happiness appeared on my mom's face, and I felt good about her acceptance.

"Oh, I'm happy and she got to be the one if she got you in here talking like this. I like this new you. Plus, I finally get to have me a grandbaby." She jumped up and down excitedly. My father looked off at nothing in particular like he had a lot to say but wasn't talking because my mom was standing right there.

"Malice, let me speak with you in the kitchen, Si?" He didn't give me an option to disagree, he was already walking away towards the hall that led to my momma kitchen. I followed suit and took a seat on the barstool while he stood behind the island facing me.

"The cartel wouldn't take Roberto seriously. You know this by the way he dresses? He cannot marry a man and expect respect within the cartel." My father folded his arms across his chest as he eyed me intensely.

"They will, plus Roberto is really delivered as he likes to say. He fucks on women and men, I guess. I don't know but I did catch him fucking the shit out of a woman in my house and I almost beat his ass for staring at my wife to long." My father looked shocked as the wheels started turning in his head. He remained quiet for a couple of seconds then spoke.

"So ju telling me, that my baby boy has relations with women? You see this with your two eyes, eh?" The look on

my father's face had me pausing trying to keep my composure but after a couple of seconds, I could no longer hold in
my laughter. We both fell out laughing hard together as my
father started to choke and cough hard. After sharing a good
laugh, we both got serious.

"I will talk to Roberto, if he is on board then I will
welcome him and demand for everyone to respect him. He
can't do all the pestering and joking that he likes to do with
you concerning the cartel. I suppose the biggest mistake I
have made as a father is the example, I set for all my kids.
Especially with you, I tried to force this on you. Now, that
you have fallen for your wife, and now I am expecting a
grandchild I'm happy that something good has came out of
all of this." I nodded my head because I agreed.

"I love your mom. She has made me suffer and pay for
my wrongs for over a decade. Now that I have her back...
I'm willing to let go of whoever to keep her. I want to do
right and live the rest of my years with the love of my life.
Don't be like me hermano, having your cake and eating it too
will leave you heart broken and lonely. Once you find the
woman that you know is for you, there is no replacing her."
My father walked around the island and placed his hand on
my shoulder.

"Just don't get my momma pregnant. I already got
enough siblings and a baby on the way. I'm not about to be
babysitting while you and ma travel the world. I know what
older wealthy folks like to do." I teased but was dead serious.
In my eyes they were too damn old to be trying to lay up and
have more kids.

"Si, that is if ju ma isn't already pregnant eh." I stood up
off the bar stool and hurried out of the kitchen. I wouldn't be
surprised if my mom ended up pregnant. They had a lot of
making up to do. The glow and smile that was plastered on

my mom's face was all the evidence that I needed to confirm that they had been back close for quite some time now.

"Your father and I not having no babies, Malice don't let him get your mind going about that." My mom was sitting on the couch, looking like she was all blushed out.

"I know ma, but if you are that's y'all business. I just want you happy." I winked and walked out of her house. My parents were back together, and I was able to tell my dad how I felt about running the cartel. I was over flying back and forth from Cali to Mexico. I could now just visit my old man and focus on my new relationship with Sovereign and my syndicate. I wanted to make sure Sovereign didn't stress because she was still leery about even carrying a baby. She kept thinking that she wouldn't be able to go full term.

With the money that I had plus good doctors, I was going to see to it that she was able to deliver a healthy baby boy, or girl. Big B was sitting on the porch playing a damn game on his phone, when he noticed me, he tucked his phone in his pocket and stood up.

"Where we headed now?" I gave him the same smile that everybody thought was mad creepy or they liked to call it sneering hard.

"I got a couple of addresses on that nigga Melvin. We about to watch that nigga and right before my wife birthday… we snatched that pussy nigga up. I think that would be the perfect birthday gift." Now all I had to figure out was how I would get her old ass Abuela to Cali. If everything worked out in my favor, Miguella, Melvin and his father would be in Hades ready to be burned alive. Sovereign would be the one to light the match.

SOULFUL HURTZ

I slept in today but woke up feeling like the weight of the world was still plastered on my shoulders. I got up and handled my hygiene and walked into the kitchen area. Grabbing the carton of orange juice, I felt a presence and quickly grabbed my nine milli from the top of the refrigerator and had it aimed soon as I shut the door with the carton and gun secured tightly pointing at my intruder.

I dropped my gun and frowned when I noticed that it was Inferno and Big B standing there with nonchalant facial expressions.

"Stay dangerous nigga, I like that... only next time shoot first check to see if a muthafucca still alive afterward." He sneered but I was used to that creepy ass look of his by now. You could look in this nigga Inferno's eyes and tell he was crazy as fuck. It was Saturday and Passion was still sleeping while I decided to let Luv go with my mom for the weekend. It was time that I let Luv see just exactly how our momma was since she wanted to defy me so badly.

Luv was now ten and for her birthday I gifted her a damn iPhone. Since she was with my mom, I called to check in on

her about a million times a day. This was my first time letting
her go and I felt like I didn't have much of a damn choice in
the matter. Luv begged to go, and my mom egged that shit on
knowing damn well she didn't need to take Luv with her. My
mom was really on her last leg with me so if anything went
down with my sister being in her custody for this weekend,
she would have to face me as the consequence mother or not.

"You couldn't just knock?" I took a seat at the dining
table and took a couple of sips from the carton as I eyed
Inferno and Big B.

"Sovereign is starting to rub off on me, you know her ass
love breaking in people's places." We all shared a small
laugh. "I don't really have much time, but I came here to tell
you about your new job."

"New job?" I frowned as I looked at him, never breaking
our stare off.

"Yes, new job Teddy." Sovereign's sweet-smelling
perfume made its way into the kitchen before she appeared.

"I want you to have more time on your hands and also put
you in a position to make good money outside of the streets. I
can't force you to go back to school nor focus back on football so I would like to make you a businessman in Inferno's
syndicate. You will be making six figures and still be something like your own boss. Training will take you about three
months, during this time you will be transforming into the
man that will be able to send your sisters to college. You
don't want them to see you dealing the same drugs that your
mom can't stay away from."

I watched her walk in front of Inferno as he pulled her
close and rubbed on her stomach. You could feel the love
between the both of them as he kept his heavy gaze on her.
The last part of what she said hit me hard and it made a lot of
sense. I kept what I did away from my sisters but there was

only a matter of time before one of them knew about what I was out in the streets doing.

"F.Y.F will always be there, but that's being taken to different lengths. I don't want you on the front-line Teddy. I want you to make better choices and follow whatever dreams and goals you come up with along the way. You still young and trust if I had the opportunity, I would have jumped on it." She looked at me somberly, and I nodded my head. I was willing to do whatever it was to still get paid.

"You can still chase your dreams baby; you just didn't have the right people in your life at the time. That's what the fuck I'm here for." Inferno kissed her temple, and I watched her blush as she smiled and turned a little to look up at him with adoration in her eyes.

"You got some kind of candy here?" Big B's deep raspy voice broke the silence as I pointed toward the pantry. Big B was a big scary looking nigga, the kind of nigga that was quiet most of the time so whenever he did speak it shocked you. He dressed funny as fuck but gave off the demeanor that would dare you to criticize him about his choice of clothes.

"What kind of work is it?" I asked curiously, I had already made a whole lot of money in the streets and had enough to hold me over.

"First, I wanted to gift you a four-bedroom house. It's going to be close to me and Malice's new house. Here are the keys." She dug into her purse and tossed me a set of keys. My heart sped up as my stomach tightened. "This is the paper-work for the house, that shit nice, and in your name. Mort-gage is going to hit you for twenty-three hundred a month, but you will be making enough a month to pay that shit up for years to come."

I hopped up and made my way towards Queen. Inferno gave us space as I pulled Queen in for a tight hug. I couldn't hold back my happy tears in front of everybody because from day one, Queen has always come through for a nigga.

"You like my family, Teddy. I know it's so much you battle, and I want you to always know I'm here for you and to show you that we always gon' be tight and more than just gang shit. I want you to be my baby's god dad. I don't really got family left, family that I even can trust but with you at least I know you someone that's solid and in my corner no matter what." We broke out of our embrace, and she took her soft delicate hands and wiped at my tears.

"We locked in for life, nigga. Yo problems is mine."

"I need your help with Luv and Passion." I was always the one that refused help. I never wanted to appear like a charity case, and I damn sure didn't want any sympathy. I was utterly confused when it came down to raising Luv and Passion. They both were way different as far as personality went. Passion hadn't been the same since she saw what she saw with our mom and Luv had nothing but anger and frustration inside of her. I felt for Passion because the mention of our mom or the sight of her made her jumpy. She didn't too much care to even be around her. It was going to take a whole lot of forgiving and understanding for Passion to even become back open to accepting Antionette.

Queen nodded her head and turned to Inferno to tell him that he could leave and that she planned on spending the day here with me. Once they were gone, Queen took off her hoodie and got comfortable. She started breakfast and had me tell her everything that had been going on with me. To say that I felt like I pushed big boulders off of my shoulders was an understatement. It felt like I released years' worth of shit that I had been holding in. Not once did Queen cut me off or stop me short of talking.

For the first time in a long time, I got a chance to express myself fully to somebody that actually wanted to hear it. She maneuvered around the kitchen effortlessly as I started talking to her about Jocelyn and how I felt about her. When I was done talking, I felt appreciative and had a whole lot of gratitude towards Queen for just listening. She sat a plate down in front of me that smelled delicious as hell. She walked back towards the counter and got another big plate that was full of different kinds of fresh fruits.

I looked down at the first plate and it had pancakes, bacon and eggs.

"I want to wake Passion up, is that okay with you? I don't want her food getting cold but before I get her... I just want to say." She took a seat next to me, the look she gave was serious.

"Never question God or blame him for how your life ended up, Teddy. That self-esteem that you're desperately looking for will come and when it do, I promise you will be very sure of yourself in so many ways that when other people talk shit about you, you won't even believe them. My esteem used to be so low that back then I would have never thought I was capable of feeling how I feel now. Can't nobody put esteem back in you but you. Our lives wasn't ideal, it wasn't typical, we had to work for shit harder than others so we appreciate the small things more then the big things. I say to you, don't question God because us imperfect humans love to question the creator. There's this thing called free will and I believe in that shit. God didn't create us as robots, and he blesses us not control us. Things happen for reasons we at the time don't understand until a time later in life comes, then we see shit clearer. You got to take small steps at accepting your-self and the hand you were dealt. I say small steps because big steps don't work right of back. Shit don't change overnight, ease your way into it, accept and don't question the blessings that's coming your way because these blessings are big as long as I'm alive. If I got it, you got it. That's my word and I stand on every word I say. Me and you ain't that far off, just a big age gap. I'm going to help you Teddy, and I can't wait to see the man you become in life. Starting with the girls, I understand you feel sorry for the situation with y'all mom. You can't let them run over you and you're the provider. The biggest mistake I made with Empress was always using our parents as an excuse for her shitty behavior. I was always giving and spoiling her, but I never thought about instilling the good traits that I had into her."

Queen looked off thinking hard on what she just said. "It's so easy to give advice but man it's often hard to follow that shit, that's why I don't like preaching to people." She cleared her throat and picked up a pineapple and chewed it. "We gon' work on the girls together, I'll even look into some counseling and see if they eventually get comfortable enough to talk to me. I'm telling you now though, I might have to whoop Luv with a belt like I had to do to yo lil bad ass when you stole from me." We both fell out laughing as Passion walked into the kitchen rubbing her eyes.

"Hey pretty girl, good morning." Queen smiled as Passion gave her a small smile back.

"Good morning, you guys." She greeted us both timidly, Passion loved to sleep in on the weekends and always took a minute to warm up once she woke up.

"Go brush your teeth and wash your face, then come eat breakfast."

Passion nodded her head and turned back around to go do as Queen instructed.

"As far as that Jocelyn chick, be her friend first then see wherever it leads. From what you telling me, she likes you Teddy. If you feel like you got too much going then be her friend, you ain't got to cut her off then get mad if she starts talking to another nigga. You a handsome young nigga. Cut your hair, groom yourself, taking small steps start with how you treat and carry yourself. Matter fact, eat this breakfast and we gone hit a couple corners. I'm going to give you a makeover today. First, we gon' feed Passion, get her dressed then head to my shop so I can give you a facial and get rid of some of those blackheads," she nudged my shoulder. Passion walked back in talkative and excited to eat breakfast. She was probably excited that she didn't have to eat cereal or burnt toast because I couldn't cook worth shit.

QUEEN, Passion and I really went on a mission when we left my house. I was happy to see Passion talking more than the short words she normally offered. She was big cheesing and looked so pretty. Queen French braided her hair and put beads at the ends. I wished Luv was with us so she could get her hair done too. When we left the house Queen stopped and got Passion ice cream and then took me straight to the barbershop. We left the barber shop and did some shopping. It felt good spending a little money. Being broke made you hold on to whatever money you made no matter how much it was. My biggest fear was struggling and not being able to buy and provide for my sisters.

Since Queen and Inferno claimed to have a job for me, I trusted that and loosened up a bit. I still didn't know what that job was, but I was appreciative for the constant cash flow. Stepping away from the streets was a big thing but I trust Queen the most and didn't want to question her judgement. We went on Rodeo Drive to her shop, and she gave me and

Passion a facial. It was nearing six o clock and we just sat down at a nice steak house and ordered some food.

My phone screen lit up and it was Luv FaceTiming me. I answered and immediately stood up out of my seat.

"Get the fuck off the phone lil bitch!" I heard my mom shouting and ran towards the exit of the restaurant.

"Tedddyyyy come get meeee please!!!!" The call ended and I felt uneasy as fuck. The look on Luv face was something I had never saw before. She looked scared and afraid the Burberry shirt I gifted her for her birthday was hanging off her little shoulders like she had been tussling. I reached for the door handle and Queen was jogging out with her phone glued to her ear. She held Passion hand as she hurriedly got in the car with a serious look on her face. We both remained quiet as I skirted out the parking lot.

Using one hand on the wheel, I repeatedly called Luv back to ease my worries. To no avail she didn't answer.

"You put your mom at the Hilton, right?" Queen typed away on her phone, I didn't have to ask, I already knew she had someone meeting us at my mom and Luv's location.

"Room five four two."

"Bet."

She reached in her purse and pulled out some apple AirPods and handed her phone and pods over to Passion.

"Listen Passion, I need you to be a big girl while we check on your sister. You can go on Netflix pick a kid movie on my phone and when we get to this hotel you stay in the car and don't step out, you understand." She has half turned around from the front seat looking directly at Passion.

"Mommy did something bad again?" Passion's voice was so soft and innocent, me hearing the worry in her tone had me gripping the steering wheel tighter as I got tunnel vision. I switched lanes and hit the freeway. I had about five minutes before I made it closer to the hotel.

"I'm not sure baby girl but me and Teddy going to make sure that Luv is okay. Do me a favor and pick a movie, put these in your ears and don't take them out."

Once Passion picked a movie, I exited off the freeway then ran a red light. I glanced over at Queen, and she had an icy look on her face.

"If I walk in that bitch and some shit looks crooked, your mom just might be taking a trip to Hades, feel me?" The look in Queen's eyes was wicked.

"What's Hades?" I raised a brow, and she offered a maniacal giggle.

"Inferno's favorite place on earth, I fell in love with it too. It's a replica of hell, except we doing the burning until they burn indefinitely in hell."

"That's my mom." My heart cracked.

"I said do you feel me, Teddy? That's yo mom, but that's a ten-year-old girl. I'm warning you if I see some shit that's far-fetched from this base head ass mother of yours, I'm putting her out her muthafuckin' misery." We pulled up to the hotel and hopped out.

Queen was already pulling the strings to her hoodie tight concealing the majority of her face. We walked through the hotel lobby holding hands probably looking crazy. When we got on the elevators, Queen pulled her gun and punched the fifth-floor button. Fear took over me, I didn't know what the fuck to expect.

The elevator dinged and Queen stepped off first and walked down the hall like she was very familiar with the hotel. Using the butt of the gun she tapped hard on the door and yelled "room service" soon as my mom cracked the door open, Queen used her shoulder ramming the door right into my mom face as she barged her way in like the police.

First thing I laid eyes on was belts and drugs on the glass table.

I saw the crack rocks and even saw fucking needles and a belt on the edge of the couch. The room was cloudy, and I couldn't even be surprised that my moms was bold enough to do this shit in front of Luv. Luv's anger bubbled over in me as I watch Queen disappear down the hallway. Placing her ear to the room door wasn't necessary because I already heard a voice that belonged to a man.

"Lil bitch, you flushed some expensive shit down the toilet." I could hear the anger in his voice as Queen looked back at me and told me to follow her lead. She turned the knob and opened up the door. Luv clothes were ripped up and she had a bruise beneath her left eye.

"Well, well…. Well. Little Peep… what's fucking good?" Queen sounded too calm as she laughed lightly. I stared at Peep with murder on my brain. What the fuck was this nigga doing in my mom room having my sister hemmed the fuck up.

"Queen? Shit I'm out in the field." He boasted as Luv ran right into my arms, she let out a loud sob and I picked her up, rocking her in my arms.

"He hit me so hard Soulful, I tried to help momma! I took those drugs and flushed them, and he gave her more and told momma he was going to make me pay for the drugs that I flushed. Momma said he was gone make me into a woman since I wanted to act grown." She shivered in my arms like she was cold, but I knew it was fear.

"Nigga you know my family! You lived next door to me in the project for years." My voice boomed.

141

"Shhhhh." Queen put her French tip index finger to her lips. "Take Luv to the living room then come right back. Luv, you're going to be a big girl and sit tight while I have a talk with your brother and Peep. Okay?" Luv nodded her head. She was such a big girl that I put her to her feet, and she walked to the living room and sat down. She didn't have any kind of reaction seeing our mother snoring on the carpet with blood leaking from her nose.

I made my way back into the room and Peep peed on himself. I don't know what Queen said to him, but he had a horrified look on his face.

"Inferno is downstairs, you're going to carry your mom down to the car with Luv. Peep you will be taking a ride with me and Inferno." Queen gave off orders, but I didn't follow as I marched right up to Peep and knocked him in the chin off his feet. I didn't stop there, I stomped him all on his chest making him choke and desperately try to catch his breath.

"You were gone make my sister a woman nigga?" Crack! I stomped him in his face.

"Teddy, enough. We have kids to think about right now." She warned and nodded her head towards the door. I stepped away breathing hard but still felt anger rumbling through me.

"I swear I wasn't." Peep murmured, making Queen laugh.

"You were Peep and you would've gotten away with it had we not arrived when we did. Now that you're bleeding, you're going to clean your fucking face in that bathroom and man the fuck up. If you want to cause a scene when we walk out this door and don't want to accept your fate easily. Then I guess I'll be peeping through your momma's house and making her and that baby momma of yours pay for all of the sins you committed tonight."

"Queen please! I've been loyal to the gang Ma." He simpered and sat up slowly.

"Loyal! The gang don't sell work to the hood nigga! Everybody knows that, then you selling to a nigga momma that's from the fuckin gang. GET YO ASS UP NIGGA AND MAN THE FUCK UP!" For the first time I heard Queen raise her voice. She got quiet when Peep stood up. He turned his back and that's when she picked her foot up and kicked him in the ass.

"Bitch ass sick nigga! That's a muthafucking kid!" I could tell she was trying her hardest to keep her composure. Her nostrils were flaring wide as she tossed a towel his way. Once his face was clean, we walked out the room. I looked down at my mom and couldn't even feel sorry for her ass anymore.

"I don't want to even look at her Queen."

"But you have to, in fact... pick her ass up. She will be signing her rights away to these girls." Luv held on to my leg and I nodded for her to go to Queen.

"Luv... you won't be seeing momma for a long time after tonight. I'm your parent and from now on you have to listen to me." I made that shit clear.

"Yes Teddy." She blinked out crocodile tears as we exited the room. My mom being in my arms was like deja vu. I made a vow that after we got her to sign her rights over, I was done with her until she really convinced me that she was clean. It was time for me to live my fucking life and raise my sisters. That's where my focus was from here on out. I was done letting my mom come in and out of our lives causing so much confusion and destruction.

The night events after the hotel were crazy. Queen and Inferno were really meant to be. They burned Peep alive down to the bones. My mom was considered dead to me until she fixed herself up and to do that could possibly take years.

Me and the girls end up spending the night with Queen and Inferno. Same night of feeling down and out, Inferno and

Queen made shit better by handing me over contracts. A contract that would change me, and my sister's life forever. Green Bay Packers was my favorite football team, I once dreamed about playing for them once I made it to the NFL.

Inferno was so well connected that he told me I didn't need an internship, but training would be for months. I was now a part of the Green Bay field operations. Queen really wanted me to end up playing but figured since I didn't want to finish school and needed to make money, she felt like this would be a good way in. I accepted and signed on the dotted line.

I used to be afraid of change but never scared to make money for the well-being of my siblings as well as myself.

SOVEREIGN

I sat in the middle of Malice's living room boohoo crying. The tears were coming down so fast I couldn't stop them. I tried to think hard on why I was even crying but so many emotions hit me as Rose moved Jack's frozen hands off the makeshift door raft. As his head disappeared into the cold ass water I rocked back and forth and cried hard shoulders shaking, nose burning with my eyes feeling heavy with more tears escaping.

"Oh, Jack!" I cried like he was my man as I reached for a sweet pickle, biting right into it then shoving some white cheddar popcorn behind it for the taste effect. I snickered a little at the fact that I was really feeling raw emotion from watching Titanic for the third time today. I was starting to realize that I had too much time on my hands now. My gang was running so smoothly without any hiccups since I had new Lieutenants in place. With the protection of the syndicate, I didn't really have to do shit but make sure I had a full-term pregnancy.

Malice was seeing to that, he had me pampered twenty-four seven. Our house was almost done being built so for now

I stayed at his Mega mansion. Some days I woke up and went straight to my shop and did work that eased my mind and served as therapy for me.

I was now four in a half month pregnant and was thrilled. The day the doctor confirmed that I was pregnant and healthy was the day I fell head over heels in love with Malice. I mean, I couldn't stand his fine ass at first and I really wasn't willing to bend for him. I got tired of running from the facts and how dainty and the soft era I was entering with her. Being with a man like Malice was a blessing and a curse. I held on to some of my independence and wasn't willing to let go of my gang because it reminded me of the savage, I had to become in order to survive.

Malice had big dick energy all the way around, from the way he walked and talked and handled his business and me as his woman. What I had with him in such a short time, I never had with any man including Melvin.

The front door opened, and I quickly wiped at my face as I got super excited to see my man walk through the door. Instead, Big B and Killa walked in with blood smeared all over their shirts. My mouth instantly went dry as I stood to my feet and watched a couple of women walk in with scrubs. Big B and Killa talked in hushed tones as Inferno walked in wearing all black. His magical-looking eyes looked dull as he offered a weak smile and then collapsed down on one knee. His deep voice rumbled with a low chuckle as he cleared his throat and forced himself to stand back up.

It was obvious that he had gotten hurt but was trying to overcome his injuries.

"Baby!" I ran towards him as he struggled and cursed at Big B for trying to help him. I quickly examined him from the top of his head to his feet until I noticed the side of his stomach. His shirt was saturated with blood. He smiled and his white teeth were covered with blood.

"I got you an early birthday gift but first, I got to let them stitch me up and get me straight." He coughed as blood leaked from his mouth. Holding on to his shirt he collapsed back down, and his face balled up in pain. Quickly fixing his face he gave direct orders as Killa and Big B listened closely.

"Sovereign, go down to the guest room." He paused and struggled catching his breath. I want you to shower; get yourself comfortable, Rosa will bring you tea and you will rest. When you wake up, I'll be good and ready to talk to you." I shook my head no, but the stern look he gave me let me know that I didn't have a choice.

Still, I stood in place as they helped him to his feet. I wanted to know if he would be okay. I didn't want to leave his side.

"I'm not some dainty ass bitch, Malice. You already know this."

"I know Sovereign, but tonight you my dainty bitch. Do what the fuck I said Sove. It's not a debate." He turned his head away and I grabbed him by the face and planted a soft kiss on his lips not really caring about the blood that decorated his sexy full lips. Even in distress, Malice looked fine as hell, and I couldn't get enough of him.

I gathered my snacks as Rosa pulled up on her golf cart helping me get my things together. This house was big enough to get lost in and I enjoyed all the amenities it came with. I couldn't wait to move into something cozier though. I didn't want to stay here were that crazy bitch Kenya frequented. I wanted a fresh start and didn't want to bring a baby in a house that Malice used as his playground. He had real corpse and bones belonging to people that wronged him and me now.

Peep's body was my first body that I watched melt and burn, and I still saw that shit vividly. Rosa made sure to take me to the other side of the house, a side I hadn't even seen. She told me that this is where Malice mother stayed whenever she came to visit, and I believed it.

This side of his home was like a mini apartment. It had a living room and kitchen with a huge bedroom with a bathroom attached. I loved the room; it had roses painted on the walls. The entire room was painted yellow and orange. Fresh flowers inside of a vase sat on the dresser. When I got to the bathroom, a bubble bath was already ready. I guess no matter what had happened to Malice tonight he had already called Rosa and had her set things up for me.

I stripped down and got in the tub but couldn't stop my thoughts of Malice. Even in his time of needing serious help he made sure I was good and that spoke a lot about how he felt about me. After spending an hour in the tub, I oiled my skin and got in bed naked. The silk sheets caressed my skin as I laid in bed alone. I scrolled through my phone and noticed I had several missed calls from Bundy.

After seeing how Kenya acted over Malice and the desperation plastered on her face. I became very careful and watchful with Bundy ass. I remember seeing the same look in his eyes when he asked me what I thought about him quitting the gang just so he could be with me. I thought back to how hard he watched me and how many times I caught him just gazing at me. We worked close together, and I trusted him when it came down to handling shit.

I just wanted to make things easier, when it came to his feelings, and I also knew I needed to be careful being with him alone. I would hate to have to shoot the nigga and kill him. I locked my phone and decided to call him tomorrow. Every night when I laid down, I thought about Abuela and

Melvin and how badly I wanted them dead before I gave birth to my baby.

Pushing those negative thoughts to the side, I gained more negative thoughts about Malice. I listened to him and came to this room because I didn't want to make shit hard for him. It was obvious that he was in pain. It also appeared that he was trying to hide something, and I didn't like the feeling of being left in the dark.

He claimed to want a real marriage, so I was confused on why I couldn't see the good, bad and ugly with him. Not thinking twice, I picked up my phone and sat up in bed and texted him exactly how I felt. At the end of the day, I was his wife and should've been in that room overseeing everything his doctor and nurses were doing to him so I could be aware of how to take care of him when they left. I texted and told him that I didn't like the way he went about things and to not let the shit happen again. I locked my phone and turned Titanic on again so I could cry myself another river with all of these pregnancy emotions I was going through.

Happy to have Rosa make me her special tea, I slowly sipped it until I drifted off to sleep. It had to be around two in the morning when I felt my bed dip. I woke all the way up consciously but still laid there playing games acting like I was fake sleeping.

Feeling Malice scoot all the way up until his thick dick laid right between my ass cheeks was a top tier feeling. He grunted like he was in pain but still pulled me as close as he could as he inhaled loudly while placing a kiss to my upper back.

"I need you to identify with your greatness instead of ya scars, Sovereign. I know you can hear me to baby, trying to lay there and act like you still sleep." He chuckled as I smiled inside still playing like I was sleep.

You gotta stop watching Titanic too, doing all this unnecessary crying, you gon' have my baby coming out being a lil crybaby. Turnover and look at me." He nudged me and kissed my shoulder. I smiled devilishly before turning to face the man that had me super hooked on him within a year.

I turned to face him and fell deeper in love. His smooth tawny golden skin shined under the dim lights. I got lost staring into his prominent magical eyes and felt like I was staring right into the eyes of my soulmate. His smokey sensual smell drifted up my nose making my eyes flutter, those burnt fingertips stroked my cheek as I picked my hand up to touch the burn mark along his jawline.

"I've been wanting to tell you for some time now that I love you Sovereign. I love everything about you from the outside to the inside. Your scars, the tattoos, the imperfect side of you down to the side that makes me sometimes believe you're perfect. I love how you talk and walk; the sex faces you make and how you make that pussy bite back when this dick snapping inside of you. I don't even give a fuck about your past and all the bodies you caught sacrificing yourself to survive. You a virgin in my eyes, cause I know for a fact can't no other nigga make this sexy ass body talk the way I do." He slapped me on the ass and rubbed the sting away.

"All I want to do is make you happy as fuck, you being happy will make me happy. You ain't defected at all, your presence is a blessing. People feel that shit, that's why muthafuccas call you Queen and your name is Sovereign because you come from Sovereignty, God's gift to the world baby. Tonight, I went to war behind you, and I promise by the end of next week your past will be erased. When you wake up in the morning, I got a gift for you. A gift that I'm ready to step up and be a man for. When you call yourself pushing me away, just know a nigga ain't never going nowhere. You gone have to kill me to force me out and away." He placed a kiss on my lips, Malice had me so speechless that all I could do was grab each side of his face and kiss him deeply.

We pulled away for air and that's when I looked into his beautiful orbs and told him the three words that I thought I would never speak to a man again.

"I love you too, Malice Ashonti Ruiz aka my burna boy." We both cracked a smile at the same time. I felt security, respect and understanding with Malice. I developed a strong compassion for him. Before I got deeper into my pregnancy, I needed to end everybody that played a part in all my pain. I didn't know what Malice meant by saying he went to war for me tonight, but the bullet and flesh wombs proved that something crazy popped off.

"What happened tonight?" I looked at him for answers.

"In the morning we will talk about everything. First, I want you to let go, I want to make love to you. In the morning, I want you to get your first early birthday gift then the next day another birthday gift. I'm gifting you all the way up until your actual birthday. I want to make this birthday rememberable for you."

Although I didn't care to celebrate my birthday and I stopped doing so years ago it felt good knowing that Malice was trying to do something special for me, so I didn't complain.

He made me want to do something special for him. He wanted to make love, but I could tell he was still in a lot of pain.

"You gon' give me the world?"

"Look at you, Sove... how can a nigga not want to give you the entire world? I'll carry that shit on my back and deliver it to you a million fuckin times if I have to."

I crashed my lips against his, then sucked on his bottom lip. I wanted to jump all over him but didn't know how bad his injuries were, so I sat up and trailed kisses down the middle of his chest. When I got down to his belly button he grunted and shook his head at me. I noticed every time I licked or kissed near his stomach he tensed up and bit into his bottom lip. I looked up into his eyes and he chuckled lowly.

"Come on baby, you tickling a nigga." He now had a silly grin on his face. I took note of it, I was for sure gone use that on him once he healed. I loved seeing Malice looking all goofy and for real smiling instead of sneering.

"You gon' teach me how to suck dick?" I raised my brows and his member stood up at attention immediately.

"Hell yea, you can't be timid with your dick though. He likes that shit nasty and sloppy as fuck." His voice deepened as I grabbed the base and placed a soft kiss to the tip of his dick.

"How nasty?" I purred and looked into his eyes as I took just his thick mushroom tip into my mouth and hummed lowly.

"I want to see spit bubbles coming out ya mouth and nose. My dick betta be soak and wet and don't suck it like you scared, suck that shit like you trying to break my shit baby." His eyes darkened as I tried to be a big girl and stuff his thick tool down to the back of my damn throat. I got halfway and started to choke and cough. Salvia gathered inside my jaws.

"Spit all that shit out and onto my dick, Sovereign." Seeing the way that he stared at me, turned me on so bad that I spit all over his dick then listened to him coach me through sucking his dick. Ten minutes into doing my thing, I felt like I was a pro.

Malice toes were cracking as he mumbled all kinds of

sexy things. His moan sounded like a deep rumble that had my pussy soaked and ready to take him all deep inside of me.

Malice came hard and when he did, I could tell he was in a lot of pain. I swallowed him down, cleaned him up then I went to wash my face and brush my teeth. Sucking his dick had me feeling victorious. Seeing him lay in the bed with low hooded eyes like he was ready to turn over and snooze had me snickering as I climbed back and bed, laying my head softly on his hard chest.

Smack!

He slapped and cupped my ass tight.

"Come sit on my dick, Sove baby." As bad as I wanted to, Malice needed to recover from his injuries. Especially the stitches I saw going across his torso. I shook my head no and pecked him on his side.

"You need to heal baby."

"Get on my dick, I didn't get shot just grazed a couple times." He shrugged like it was nothing. "Come on, Sove. That pussy wet and my dick can sense it, look." He made his dick jump; I giggled and rolled my eyes. Sitting up, I slowly got on top of him.

Lustful passion took over me as I eased down his dick. We were in a stare off that couldn't be broken as I placed my hands flat on his chest and finished easing all the way down. Filling me to capacity, I cried out softly and started rotating my hips.

"Fuck, Sovereign." My pussy tightened, my breathing became heavy, mind cloudy as I went up and down, round and round riding him like my life depended on it.

"Do yo shit, sexy muthafucka." Malice grabbed my breast and grunted out as I picked up the pace.

His dick felt so good inside of me that I couldn't even utter a single damn word. Malice gripped my chin, tilting my gaze to him. I was close to my first climax, and it was hard to keep my eyes open. His breaths were hard and heavy. My body was trembling, pussy pulsating, I became mindless.

"Yes!!!" I gasped out loudly as my skin smacked against his pelvis. He frowned his face up and leaned forward a little. Kissing me softly and tilting my head back as he stared at my neck. Licking from my shoulders to the middle of my neck, chills had me shuddering and shaking on his dick as I felt my orgasm hitting hard.

I swallowed harsh breaths as my pussy tightened on his dick.

"Choke my shit, baby." He slapped me on the ass. It felt like I was losing my mind and sanity right in his arms.

"You gotta cum again on my dick baby." He pleaded and I heard him, my body just couldn't stop shaking and I couldn't catch my damn breath.

Gripping my hips tightly, I knew Malice was ready to take over and pummel my pussy until it died, and he would be forced to revive it.

I inhaled his scent and let him take control. His movements were slower, and I knew it was because of his wombs and the pain he was probably feeling.

He got comfortable between my thighs, heart pounding in my ears, I anticipated what was to come. My thighs spread wide for him; I was damn near doing the splits to receive him greedily. Malice cupped my pussy like a stress ball, leaning his hard body against my breast, he kissed along my jawline as he strummed my swollen clit.

"Look how wet this fat pussy is for daddy." He dug two fingers deep inside of me, making my pussy talk disrespectfully. Fuck, I was losing it. Malice never rushed when he handled my body. He explored every inch and was determined to see how my body responded to everything he did.

"Tell me what you want Sovereign." His eyes darken, voice deepens with need. He picks up the pace of how his fingers worked my inside, teasing my G spot, I cry out.

"You!" I moan breathlessly.

"Be more specific." He drags his fingers from inside of me and circles my clit with added pressure.

"I want you, inside of me Malice!" I can feel the tears ease out the corners of my eyes.

"Okay baby." He commanded so much of me, and he knew it. My heart skipped a beat as he aligned his dick with my soppy wet tunnel and slid into the hilt.

"Pussy biting." He mumbled. "This shit crazy, Sovereign. I'm your got damn groupie. I'm hooked, I'm addicted to you. You my number one." He delivered long strokes as he shook his head and chuckled. "Pussy got me talking crazy, baby." I couldn't respond because I was too choked up.

Kissing me from my mouth to my jawline then collarbone, I savored every second of it.

"Mines." Was all he said, and I felt even his words because he was mines too. I opened my legs to receive more of him. Tracing my fingers down my chest, pass my belly button. I touched my clit and circled my bud as he pushed in and out of me. My second orgasm flowed through me hard hitting harder than tsunami. Sliding my fingers free, I clamped my thighs hard around him trying to ride the wave, but Malice didn't ease up.

Sliding his big, rugged hands underneath my ass, he grabbed each ass cheek as leverage and pounded into me relentlessly. Malice snarled and slid out slowly as my body jumped from being sensitive, he pushed back in even harder, knocking the wind out of me. This is what I meant by him reviving my pussy and then re killing it again.

I wound my arms around him as I locked my legs around

his buttocks, twisting my hips and fucking him back, had him demanding me to cum one more time on his dick and I obeyed. I came hard riding a blissful wave as he nutted deep inside of me. His growls turned into harsh breaths as he collapsed on the side of me, pulling me close. We said nothing as we both let sleep take over us.

I woke up the next morning still feeling sex high. I looked around and smiled because Malice had a dozen teal blue flowers laying in his empty spot. My body tingled all over as I picked up my phone and looked down at the time. It was nearing noon; I couldn't even believe that I actually slept that long.

I showered and checked my messages and missed calls. I had a couple of calls from Bundy again as well as a few other members from F.Y.F. Looking at myself in the mirror, I blushed at all the hickies between my breast leading all the way up to my neck and collarbones. I had marks all over my body, my lady parts were aching. I needed a trip to the spa for a good massage and just to relax for a day or two.

I texted Bundy, letting him know that he and I would meet later today after I figured the location. It was time for me to sit him down along with Teddy. I would arrange a meeting to let the rest of the team know that Teddy was no longer apart of F.Y.F. Bundy was probably wondering where did Peep disappear to. I would explain that to but for now, I needed to find Malice in this big ass house. He had a lot of explaining to do.

After putting my lotion and perfume on, I slipped on my Fendi jogger suit with the matching shoes. After applying a thin coat of clear gloss, I was satisfied with my look. I didn't look pregnant at all. It actually looked like I lost weight.

"I can page Rosa; I figure me and you can take a walk before we meet with your special guest." I turned to look at

Malice, he looked relaxed and handsome as hell. I learned that Prada was his favorite clothing brand. The pieces that he chose to wear from Prada always fit him perfectly. Today he had on plain tan pants with a brown and tan Prada shirt.

I hope he kept his wild short curls; his lineup was crisp and so was his goatee. He approached me appearing normal as hell like he didn't stumble in the house yesterday. His walk was normal, like he wasn't in any type of pain either.

"Tell me what happened, yesterday." He covered my lips with his, making sure to bite down softly on my bottom lip. Just like that, I was ready to pull my Fendi sweats down and arch my back for him. Malice looked and smelled good as hell.

"Cuba, is what happened. I needed to get my woman closure from all past situations. So, I started with the daughter you unrightfully took from your ex-wife." He held his hand out for me to grab but I stood frozen in place. What did he do?

"Melvin sold the little girl for a hefty penny. She was sold to one of the biggest underground sex trades in Cuba." He paused as my knees buckled at the mere thought of every-thing Princess had to go through from just a baby. I took a seat at the edge of the bed and steadied my breathing.

"Her name is Acindina, the tranquil name means Safe." My heartbeat turned back normal a little bit as I continued to listen to him.

"A family adopted her. A family that comes from a lot of money so when Big B and Killa plus myself approached the mobsters house, he stuck his men and dogs on me." Malice chuckled then continued. "Nothing can deter me when I'm determined for something you know that. So, I had to prove to Neosa that I meant no harm to his daughter and wife."

"Princess is my daughter." I stood up ready to face whoever I had to face to get her back.

"She is not your daughter, the kid in your stomach rightfully belongs to you, Sovereign. Now we straightened some things out and Neosa is willing to let you be involved with Acindina. He knows her past and is very protective of her.

"You can't tell me what the fuck it is, Malice!" Anger consumed me. He walked up on me, towering over my short frame like a giant.

"Yes, the fuck I can, calm yo ass down and do that shit fast. You know how I view my time. I'm trying to be understanding but that ugly ass attitude and you not having understanding is gone fuck it all off." I calmed down a bit, even though my rage could go up, Malice rage was hot.

"You had that baby cut out of an innocent woman that had no clue who you were to her husband. At some point, you have to take accountability. You never had someone who loves you like I do to make you realize your wrongs." It felt like he was using a knife to drag it down the center of my chest. I knew what he was saying was real and indeed true, but it pained me.

"I wanted to hurt Melvin," I whispered as he tilted my chin upward. Pecking me on my nose he looked at me sincerely.

"I understand, in the line of business of what we do things like this happens. I just need for you to understand the facts. Acindina is a child that will grow into an adult. Neosa her adoptive father doesn't know what you did to her real mother all he knows is that Melvin took her from you, and she was about to be traded once she was sold as a baby. Neosa wife always wanted kids, so he took her and adopted her. You cannot take her away or try to create a war behind her when we are leaving the cartel behind us. Do you understand what I'm saying to you baby?"

I somberly nodded my head yes, if I could just see her one time and see with my own two eyes that she was fine that would do me good.

I looked up at Malice and wanted to break down in cry. This man was righting my wrongs and risking his life to make sure I had the closure that I needed to move on throughout life and focus on what was now important.

"Thank you, baby." I threw my arms around him struggling on my tippy toes until he leaned down and pulled me close up against him.

"This is only the beginning, now come on so you can meet Acindina. She thinks you are her aunt on her father's side. She's a very sweet girl and her mannerisms are good. Try not to get too emotional in front of her." He grabbed my hand as we headed for the door. Nervousness and excitement took over me. Malice was the man for doing this.

MALICE

*J*leaned up against the wall in Hades, pulling out my twenty-four karat lighter I flicked it on and off. I watched the flames dance before my eyes and couldn't wait to watch my wife's enemies burn so we could move forward.

"She will never kill me!" I turned and smiled at Empress. What she said was true, but I wasn't the one to have to chance shit or double back. I wasn't wasting any more time on none of these muthafuckas.

I looked around the room and eyed everyone down. It was easy capturing Melvin. If I didn't get to him Neosa would have for the sake of Acindina.

"Queen will never forgive you for killing our father! She loves us she's just mad right now!" Empress just couldn't be quiet.

"Shut up bitch! For melt your fucking mouth shut." I chuckled watching Empress shutter. She simpered and looked at her weak-ass daddy for help. I paid so much money on jet fuel traveling and snatching muthafuckas up. These five stupid muthafuckas thought shit was sweet until it turned sour as fuck. I looked over at Miguella and cringed at the sight of her. The first thing I had Roberto do to test his gangsta was annihilate the entire Martinez cartel.

I told him to leave Miguella alive, but they did a number on her old frail ass. She put up a hard fight and even tried to shoot her way to freedom. She even tried her best to protect Melvin's dad but failed. Soon as I saw Roberto bust his gun wearing an all-black custom-made tailored suit that fit him tight as hell with a pink mink coat dragging to the ground. It took everything in me to keep a straight fucking face.

I looked over at Melvin's father who sat right next to his son, his focus was on the love of his life Miguella. From the sad look in his eyes, he didn't give a damn about himself. All he cared about was her well-being and it showed just how far he would go for the sick evil bitch.

"If it was left up to me, you all would be burning right now. However, my wife will have the pleasure in doing all of that. Right now, she's up there with the daughter you sold." Melvin eyes turned into tiny slits he moved a little and I turned my eyes towards Killa dumb ass.

"What?" He shrugged and took a pull from his blunt.

"Nigga what? I told yo dumb ass to tie him tight enough so he couldn't fuckin' move, that's what nigga." Big B chuckled and moved towards Melvin and tightened the rope at his feet then moved towards his upper body. The stench in here was pungent, Miguella shitted on herself soon as she was tied down to the chair.

"Get some water and soap and drenched that bitch." I pulled my cigar out and lit it.

"Nigga you got something to say?" I looked at Melvin and smiled. "Save those words for Sovereign, not me. You say the wrong shit to her and upset her while she's pregnant with my baby, I'm gone torture you before she burns you." I warned, and his eyes got big at the mention of her being pregnant.

"Matter fact, Big B, take the tape off him and put some on that bitch." I pointed towards Empress. I pulled my phone out and called Sovereign. I was losing track of time. It was past the time of her visit with Acindina. I knew my wife well; she didn't sit around waiting on me. She understood that I always had business to tend to. She checked in with me and let me know when she was ready for me to be home and I abided by that shit. I also knew that she had business as well, I didn't want to be controlling when it came to her, but I also liked to know where she was and who she was near. Protecting her and my baby meant the world to me.

"Where you at?" Sovereign loved to answer the phone and not say shit. She always waited for the person that was calling her to talk first. If she called, you she sometimes would wait for you to greet her then rudely get to the point. My wife, my beautiful fuckin wife. I loved everything there was to her complicated ass.

"Meeting with Bundy, I took Teddy with me. We at Seaside Steak House. I'll be home in a couple of hours." Melvin chuckled lowly and I snapped my eyes towards him.

"Okay. I'll see you soon." She hung up and I marched over to where Melvin sat.

"You got something to say nigga?" I blew smoke in his face. Even knowing that he was about to soon die the nigga was bold as fuck.

"I just can't wait to lay eyes on Sovereign. I fucked up bad with her, following those two orders." He nodded toward his father and Miguella. Miguella was out of it snoring loudly.

"I'll die a happy man soon as I see all those fucking curves and ass. Hopefully my brother Bundy takes her fine ass off your hands." He laughed while looking amused. I guess he figured he was getting under my skin. That was true too. Only difference was, he was the nigga strapped down to a chair not me.

I sniggered right along with him until my smile dropped. I picked my foot up and kicked him dead in the mouth, his head whipped back. He laughed like the joker and spit out two front teeth. Putting my cigar out on his forehead, I let it drop to the ground and two pieced him in the face, enjoying the sound of my fist breaking his nose and splitting his lip.

"YOU GOT SOMETHING TO SAY TO ME ABOUT MY WIFE NIGGA?!" I roared, I felt myself losing control and that was bad. I was trying my hardest to leave this nigga alive for Sovereign. He chuckled and winced out in pain. Giving me a lopsided grin, he muttered.

"No matter how much pussy I got after or during my time of being with her. None of those bitches compared. Her pussy was so sweet, so fuckin' tight. If I was loose, I'd try my best to kill you nigga. THATS MY BITCH FOREVER! EVEN AFTER DEATH!" He spat out a mouthful of blood on my Prada loafers. I looked over at Big B and clicked my teeth twice. Killa shook his head at me, but I ignored him.

"I think I've been too fuckin' nice! Drench that niggas crotch area. Something tells me when he see my wife, he gone get a hard on. The best way to fix that is to melt this niggas dick." Melvins eyes bulged out his head as Big B poured the lighter fluid all over his crotch area.

"When my wife get here, I'm gone burn you so bad nigga that there won't be a life after death." I snarled.

"Wait, hold up." He attempted to move but couldn't as his mouth leaked blood like a broken faucet.

"Too late." I lit the match and dropped it on his pants. Soon as the flames ignited, he screamed loud as fuck waking

Miguella up, and prompting her shitty ass to scream right along with him.

I stood in front of the flames, embracing my dark side. The fire was so alluring that I couldn't blink. The flame rose higher scorching his chin as it dazzled my senses. The fire twirled and danced before my eyes, and I watched very closely until Killa walked up with a fire extinguisher and put it out. I frowned down at Killa ready to light his ass up next. Melvin was passed out with half of his dick melted in his lap.

"Now you gotta present these muthafuckas to Sovereign early. This nigga ain't gone live past six to seven hours max." Killa reasoned.

"Good, go get my wife and make sure Bundy is with her." Big B was the first to walk out of the room. Killa followed as I went to take a seat in the corner of the room. I don't know how I let that get past me. Bundy being this nigga's half-brother. I planned on killing Bundy soon as he walked through the door. I wasn't giving his lying ass the option to explain shit to Sovereign.

Anybody related to Melvin had to go, except Acindina. I was glad after today Sovereign chose to close that chapter with Melvin's daughter. To me, it was playing things to close. Suppose she got older and wanted to seek revenge. It was best to let the little girl live her life and not know much about her past. The little girl was fortunate to be alive with a bitch ass biological father like Melvin. Niggas like him only gave a fuck about themselves.

I needed air, this room was starting to suffocate the fuck out of me. I shot Rosa a text and told her to make me a tea that would boost my energy. If I didn't control myself better, I could easily see myself laying everyone in this room down. No one inside of this room had a logical answer or fair enough excuse to why they did Sovereign the way that they did.

I went up the steps of Hades and closed the door. Walking through my room, I met Rosa at the door to get my tea from her. Soon as I made my way down the steps, my eyes landed on Sovereign's father. I thought back to the conversations that Sovereign and I had regarding her dad, and she still loved him. She even mentioned how she was happy that he was alive and how it was going to take time for her to forgive him for just disappearing on her.

I didn't trust the nigga at all but because of my wife, I had plans of untying him now. I had to show this nigga that I didn't give a fuck who was who, if you wronged my wife, you would be dealt with. Taking a couple of sips from my hot ass tea, I ignored the feeling of the hot liquid burning the ridge of my mouth as well as my tongue. I had been moving around taking care of shit for days in a row with little to no rest.

Rosa tea always gave me the extra energy boost that I needed.

"Miguel?" I sat my tea down and picked up a long blade. "I'm gon' let you free so we can talk man to man. That treacherous daughter of yours is staying tied up until my wife gets home. Don't think for one second, you can risk your life, once I cut you free." He somberly nodded his head, and I started cutting the rope to free him. I hope he took my warning and planned on listening to that shit.

I wouldn't mind knocking his old ass the fuck out and explaining to my wife how bold of a father she had. I led him to my bedroom and took a seat on my lounge couch. He looked around lost for a minute then finally took a seat on the love seat across from me.

We had a silent stare off saying nothing. The longer I

stared at him, I could see a lot of resemblance between him and Sovereign. Sovereign took after her mother's complexion, making her look like she was fully black, her curly silk hair gave away the fact that she was mixed. She shared the same nose as her father and those light brown eyes as well.

"Young man, I have nothing to explain to you. I owe it to my daughters, the only thing I've done that I regret tremendously is leaving my girls to fend for themselves. I was so stuck on my heart being broken that I disappeared and cried ever since my Sovereignty was killed. All I want is to get back right with both of my girls and it's killing me seeing them at odds although Empress is all the way wrong. I've been respecting my daughters request by giving her space." I nodded my head at his honesty and him taking accountability for his actions.

"I only kidnapped and tied you down so you can see that when it comes to my wife, I won't stop at nothing when it comes to her peace and protection." He released a breath, looked around my room then back at me. I could tell he was growing nervous by the way his Adams apple kept moving up and down his throat.

"No, she won't kill Empress. If she wanted to, I wouldn't stop her. She loves that girl too much to even think about killing her." I stated, disappointingly. He looked relieved until Sovereign entered the room with Bundy following closely behind looking like a lovesick puppy. Killa and Big B were standing outside of the door along with my other men.

I would've killed Bundy right where he stood right now but didn't want to mess up my freshly polished floors.

"Papa? What you doing here?" Sovereign frowned in confusion. Miguel stood and she walked right into her father's arms. I can tell she was going through different emotions but tried her best to conceal them.

"Your father and I needed to talk." I stood up keeping my eyes on Bundy.

"What's going on Malice?" Sovereign voice was so damn sexy. Shit, everything about her was raw and authentic. She was truly a blessing to whoever she offered her presence to.

"I told you that I was going to place everyone that had wronged you in the same room. We were going to burn them, and you would forget all about them." I looked deep into her eyes and grabbed her soft hands into mine.

"I told you that I would handle all of that in due time, Malice." She squeezed my hands. I could see the excitement in her eyes, still she tried to play shit cool.

"Bundy?" I kept looking into Sovereigns eyes as I called this niggas name. He didn't answer, that was cool.

"When we're you going to tell my wife that you are Melvin's brother." Sovereign gave a faint gasp as she turned fast on her feet and slapped the betrayal from Bundy's face.

"Get that nigga comfortable in Hades." I clicked my teeth as Killa and Big B man handled him. He shouted and screamed until Big B's big ass knocked him unconscious. Throwing him over his shoulder we watched the men disappear into my closet.

"What you need to understand all the way Sovereign is that you belong to me. I love you; I've expressed how I felt. So, tell me, how can a man express himself and show how deeply in love he is, if I'm still letting you roam and take care of some shit that your husband should be doing?" I stepped into her personal space forgetting that her father was standing close by. Grabbing her by the waist, I pulled her against my body and inhaled her scent deeply.

"Don't insult me again, by telling me what you can handle on your own. Shit like this ain't up for debate." I leaned down and close to her ear so only she could hear me.

"Keep the pussy tight and clean for me, that's the only thing I see you doing for yourself, if you need help with that, I don't mind." I chuckled into her ear and stood tall watching her pretty ass blush and squirm right in front of me. I smacked her softly on the ass and stepped away from her. If I continued, then I wouldn't be able to keep my dick under control.

"Who's all down there?" She tilted her head looking up at me.

"Melvin, his father, your sister and Miguella, Bundy is now added to that." She gave me a pleased smirk and started pacing back in forth like she didn't know what to do with herself.

"This is one of my birthday gifts?" She exclaimed not holding back that big, beautiful smile of hers. When she smiled really hard you could see the dimples on each side of her cheeks.

"Yes baby." She ran and jumped in my arms; I couldn't help but to grab a handful of ass. She grazed her lips against my ear and now it was her turn to whisper some sexy shit into my ear.

"I'm sucking the black off that dick tonight." She purred and blew into my ear. I had to turn away from her father because all the blood rushed straight to my dick.

"I'm holding you to that shit." I tried to put her down, but she kept her legs clamped tight around me.

"I want you to carry me down the steps and into Hades." She wound her arms tight around my neck and pecked my lips.

"Alright, but when the fire starts, you got to leave." She nodded her head in agreement.

I walked her towards Hades and her father stopped us.

"Sovereign?" He carefully called her name.

"I'm not killing her Pa." She was referring to Empress.

"Let me kill, Miguella." Sovereign froze, like she was thinking it over.

"Okay." Was all she offered. I carefully walked down the steps with Sovereign holding on to me with her head lying comfortably on my shoulder. When we got to the last step, all eyes were glued to us, and Sovereign went into action.

I put her down to her feet and she walked right up to Empress. She slapped her a couple of times until she saw blood leaking from her mouth. She eyed her sister carefully as Empress cried out in pain.

"I don't know if I can ever forgive you, you're dead to me Em. Let her go y'all." I nodded at Big B, and he marched towards Empress letting her out of the rope. When she was free, she collapsed to Sovereign's feet and pleaded hard with her. Sovereign kicked her sister right in the face making her yelp and spit out the tooth that was hanging from her gums.

"I love you, Sovereign." Empress went right to her dad, and he consoled her as she cried in his arms.

"GET OUT!" Sovereign's voice boomed. She looked like the cold calculated woman that I first met.

I entered my bedroom and walked straight to my walk-in closet. Removing the frame and then pushing my safe out the way, I unlocked the hidden door that would lead me down the steps of my chamber. Soon as the door opened, I braced myself for the feisty woman that had piqued my interest a little. She was a fighter and stood firm on all ten toes. I thought by the second day of being held in Hades she would surely cave in and fold, but she welcomed it. She fought me hard each time my hidden door opened. Although she was no match for me, I loved the hard effort she put up.

Her arms swung wildly as I stepped to the side and grabbed her by the base of her neck. I sunk my sharp pinky nail deep into her neck until it penetrated and put her in shock.

"Simmer the fuck down, if I let you go and you swing again. Be prepared to tumble your ass down those flight of steps."

Silence.

The only thing that I heard was her heavy breathing.

"I can't breathe good down here, I need air." The only light that illuminated the top steps to my chamber was from my closet.

Her soft voice was replaced now with a slight rasp from all the ashes and dust that surrounded her. I was sure that her throat was burning, and she was in need of a shower and a hot meal. I wasn't all the way heartless. I had my guard bring her food and water and I knew the max number of days that she could be held captive in my chambers without collapsing or having major health problems.

"I'm going to let you come out, take a shower, eat and then we will talk business. I'm pretty sure now you are ready to comply. Right?"

"Fuck you." She huffed as I squeezed her neck tighter. My dick stiffened against her stomach as I brought her closer. Leaning down so I could speak directly in her ear, I could feel her chest rising and falling and her once steady breathing became choppy and shallow breaths were now being taken.

"I would fuck you. I'd fuck you so good that you'd forget all about your title as a struggling Queenpin." I looked down and smiled at her clamping her thighs tight. The rebellion was locked in her eyes. I wouldn't press her any further.

"Try to run and the men outside my door have been ordered to shoot first, then check in with me after," I warned as I stepped to the side to let her by. I had been careless with showing her Hades. No one entered this part of my house or

even visited my room. Anytime Kenya came over she remained on the opposite wing. Sovereign stood in my walk-in closet as I locked the heavy door and moved everything back into place.

"Come." I moved past her and went to sit on the chaise in front of my bed.

"Strip down." I stared at her intently, I tried to read the tattoos that were scattered about on her smooth-looking toffee skin. The tattoo that stuck out the most was the one along her collarbone that said, "Man Eater." I stared into those deep hazel brown orbs of hers and also noted the tiny, shattered heart tattoo right on her high cheekbone that must have been easily covered with makeup. The two tear drops tatted on the opposite side of her face could have meant multiple things.

She had a story and she been through some heavy shit, it was the main reason why she didn't act like a damsel in distress being snatched up by me. She didn't have an ounce of fear within her. She didn't jump at the sound of my voice, and she was currently standing with her hands on her hips like she didn't just hear what the fuck I just ordered her to do.

"Strip, Sovereign." I hated repeating myself.

"You know if you let me out of this hell dungeon of yours, I'm going to kill you. Usually, when people learn my name, they meet their fate. So, what's yours?" All the blood rushed to the head of my dick. I looked at her dry plump lips and traced every curve that she had with my eyes. Even with her looking crazy and her wild curly hair all over her head, she was beautiful as fuck. Bolder than a nigga with a gun stuck to his head and talking shit. I was stuck on my own words for the first time ever. Sovereign was a bloodhound, she noticed me being stuck and continued her assault.

"You got some sexy ass lips and eyes, kind of remind me

of my twins that I enjoy from time to time. Nah, your look is more exotic, it looks like you one of those freaky mothafuckas, that's why you want me to strip and shit." A look of amusement crossed her face and then her face was void of emotion. She was very good; she had the gift of gab and confidence reeked straight from her pores. She kept her eyes locked in with mine unwavering as she stripped out of her top and then skirt. She slid her panties down slowly until they formed into a puddle around her bare feet.

She turned around and bent over to pick up her clothes and I stood to teach her a fucking lesson. Sovereign was fuckin with the wrong nigga. I was the nigga that would bring her down to her knees and have her going to a shrink to be evaluated to make sure she was sane. I was the nigga that she would daydream about during the day while conducting business. I would be in her nightmares and wet dreams every single night when she closed her eyes. Her pussy lips glistened, and no foul smell permitted the air.

"Stay just like that and don't move Sovereign." My voice came out husky as I moved to my dresser to retrieve a condom. I pulled my dick out and protected myself. I eyed the rolls on her back and all the stretch marks that decorated her thighs like tiger strips and let out a grunt. I never expected my dick to react to a woman of her size, but I was about to find out what this feeling was all about.

I grabbed the top of her ass and let my dick guide its way inside. There was no slow lovemaking or trying my very best to ease in slowly. Sovereign talked big shit so she should have been prepared to take a big dick with hard long strokes in her snug, shit! Just the tip was in, and my toes curled so tight that they started to cramp. Forcing my thoughts back on the lesson that I was teaching, I pushed all ten inches halfway in before she fell to the floor on her knees howling like she was a virgin.

"What's wrong, Sovereign? You can't take dick?" I got down on my knees behind her and gripped her waist, pulling her back up and entering her again. Every time I got halfway in, she ran, and I couldn't hold back my chuckle. She smelled like fire mixed with burned ashes which made my dick even harder. I pictured me fucking her right in Hades while the flames crackled around us.

"Yea, you can't take dick baby girl. I ain't into teaching a woman how to take my dick. Next time, watch your fuckin mouth and do as I say." I slapped her on the ass and stood to my feet. Snatching the condom off, I tossed it into the small trash bin. I left her right on the floor panting and trying to save face.

What she didn't understand and what I didn't understand was that she ignited some weird shit that I couldn't explain. I dropped it, that feeling was dangerous and something I couldn't be pondering on. I vowed to never stick my dick inside of her snug tunnel again. I thought about the smart remarks of her claiming to fuck twin brothers and a dark thought crossed my mind. This woman was not mine, she would soon be working under me and paying a percentage for the syndicate's protection.

She wasn't even my type of woman, don't get me wrong, I've seen a couple of big girls that looked good and carried themselves even better. Sovereign took the whole cake of that; she looked damn good and dangerous. She knew how lethal she was and what drew me in to her was her ability to keep on fighting.

She wasn't some delicate bitch that caved in when it came to being pressured. When she looked at me, she had the same stare that I gave plenty of people. In a creepy way it felt like I was staring at the woman version of me. The wheels in my head started to spin, this woman could very well bring millions to the table.

Now I didn't give a damn what she could bring to the table, I only wanted her and all of her. I knew from the very first time I entered her that I was hooked on her. That's why I didn't even deny my feelings for her. Once she opened up to me about everything is when I found myself falling deeper in love with her. God didn't just make women like her on the regular, so when or if you came across a woman like Sovereign the best thing to do was treat her exactly what her name stood for.

Empress left out of Hades, and I hope she left my home. Sovereign reached for her gun and pulled out a beautiful teal chrome nine-millimeter. She walked right up to her Abuela and snatched the tape off.

"You always said, I was such a classless black bitch. Member, you wanted to try some of the same dick me and Empress was sharing? Now that was some classless shit for you to do Abuela don't you think?" Miguella gathered what-ever spit she could inside her mouth and even her aim was weak. The spit that was supposed to land on Sovereign dripped down her chin. Sovereign looked at me and doubled over in laughter.

She laughed so hard that tears fell down her cheeks. Without looking at Melvin's father she kept her eyes on Miguella and shot the nigga in the side of his head. I had to walk to the corner of my chambers in take a seat because that was some sexy ass shit.

"Ju, perra Negra!!!!!" (You black bitch!) Miguella cried out like her soul had left her body. So, the evil bitch was in love after all, she could no longer look at Sovereign, she cried like she was dying, her cries bounced off the walls as Sovereign spoke above her cries.

"Now that's some classless ass shit, Abuela. See, that's the way my Pa been crying since you had that same nigga leaking over there kill my momma." Sovereign's voice cracked a little. She cleared her throat and kept talking.

"You heard what I said? That's some classless shit Abuela, or should I say Miguella! Look at you, all broken down and shit. Looking stupid as fuck! What you say to me back at your house in Mexico?" Sovereign placed the gun to her ear like she was waiting on an answer. Miguella was so far gone in her crying that she kept her eyes locked on Melvin's father.

"I'm sorry." Miguella cried out. "Sovereign, please wake him up." She finally looked at Sovereign and started pleading out hard.

"I think this bitch got dementia." Sovereign giggled and mumbled to herself, giving Miguella an icy look. "Can you go wake my momma up bitch? Please! Go wake up Sovereignty and then I'll wake up this nigga. DO IT! Wake my momma up bitch!" I went to go stand next to my wife so she could feel my presence close to her. I didn't want her breaking but I could hear it in her voice that she was close to getting emotional.

Miguel walked up to his daughter and grabbed the gun out of his daughter's hand and emptied the clip right into his mom. He turned and pulled Sovereign into his arms but like the Queen she was she stood up straight and took the gun from her father and went to approach Melvin. This shit was getting good. Killa walked up to Sovereign with a big smile on his face. He handed Sovereign his gun as her eyes went right to Bundy.

"Queen, listen to me, I never fucked with this nigga! I love you Queen and I understand that you don't look at me like that, I respect you for it and –" Two shots to the head for Bundy. Sovereign was on a roll, and I loved every minute of this shit. When we were done in Hades, I was running my wife a hot bubble bath and massaging every inch of her skin. She handed Killa the gun back and made her way towards Melvin.

"Hi Melvin." She sweetly sang it like she was about to do something nice for him. Snatching the tape from his mouth she laughed right in his face.

"I see my husband already introduced himself as Inferno." She looked down at his burned skin as he weakly looked into her eyes trying his hardest to muster a smile. I had to give it to the nigga, he didn't back down and he already took his fate to the chin. Nigga knew he was a dead man walking and didn't want to appear weak even in his last minutes of being amongst the living.

"I don't have much to say, and I don't even want to elaborate on shit with you, nigga. All I can say is thank you for fucking up and betraying me. If you didn't, I wouldn't be hooked on the king of Cali. See you around Melvin." She lifted her sweatpants a little and pulled another gun from her right ankle that was holstered to her leg. Soon as she stood up, she shot him between the eyes until her gun clicked indicating that she emptied the clip.

Grabbing my hand, she kissed my jaw and thanked me as I walked her towards the steps.

"Don't stay in here too long." She told me smiling, she looked refreshed and happy. "I want to thank you for the best birthday gift ever." I leaned down and kissed her slowly and watched her climb the steps with her father, Big B and Killa right behind her. Once everyone was gone, I looked down and saw the trail of lighter fluid. Big B was already ahead of the game and that's why he was my nigga and got paid well.

"From ashes to ashes, dust to dust." I smirked and lit my cigar with a match, dropping it, I watched the fire travel to each body that was tied down to a chair and ignite with fire. Sure, this was a gift to Sovereign, but it felt like a gift to myself in the end.

SOVEREIGN

THREE MONTHS LATER

*W*hen I woke up this morning in Jamaica, it felt like I was dreaming. That's how shit felt every damn morning. I woke up to a man that I was head over hills in love with. Malice and I sat under a cabana. I watched him tote on his cigar looking fine as hell. His mom and dad chased each other on the beach like long-lost lovers. My eyes traveled further down the sand until they landed on my father. He was constantly back in forth between here and Mexico.

Empress and my father picked up right where Abuela left off at with the cartel. He made sure to come to visit me every other month and each time he came he came with gifts and more apologies. I had to tell him to stop apologizing and just be my father. What was done was done and I was over everything that had happened to me.

The day Malice set my past on fire was the day I let all of my pain and anger burn right along with them. I no longer held on to that shit I let it go especially since none of them posed as a threat to me anymore. This was our third day in Jamaica and Malice made the shit ten times sweeter. He set up a real wedding with just our immediate family, my father walked me down the aisle and Teddy's little sisters were my flower girls.

I was so proud of Soulful, he had done a three-sixty. Got his high school diploma and was now in college. He took the job for the Green Bay Packers and just like me and Malice had figured they convinced him to follow his dreams. He still was in training but once they saw that he actually had good skills they offered him a spot on the team, and he took it. I couldn't wait to see him play. I helped him as much as I could with the girls. The first time I watched Luv and Passion, Luv pulled that "You ain't my momma" card and I whooped her little ass and got her right in line.

F.Y.F practically ran itself, I had Killa running things the gang was basically under the syndicate. They were eating well, and I was happy that I didn't leave my gang hanging. Most of them came to see me at my shop, I enjoyed popping blackheads and giving facials.

"You so damn sexy." Malice licked his lips as I felt our baby girl kick hard at hearing her dad's voice. My baby would be due in another month, and I couldn't wait to lay eyes on her.

"I know." I blushed, picking up my coconut to take a couple of sips of my new favorite drink. Before I could remind Malice of what it was we had to do tomorrow morning. Roberto came strutting on the beach with a whole bunch of company. I burst out in a fit of laughs as the older people frowned at him.

Their frowns made him switch his hips harder. He had on a light blue bikini with an elephant-looking trunk flapping down his thigh.

"The fuck you staring at, Sovereign?" I laughed even harder at Malice's jealous acting ass. It wasn't my fault his brother was blessed and the flamboyant men he brought to the ocean were just as hung as him. He had some beautiful women with him too. Roberto looked like new wealth from a great distance, and I was happy for his crazy ass.

We talked on the phone just about every day, his drama was entertaining but beyond that he was someone that I enjoyed spending time with and talking shit with.

He came into the cartel shaking shit up and I loved how uncomfortable he made certain ones that weren't secure with their own sexuality. Roberto loved fucking men as much as he did women. He was also a nurturer. For his birthday I bought him an all-pink Ak-forty-seven.

He put his private jet to great use, and I was happy Malice gifted him one for his birthday. Malice complained the whole time getting his special gift. He had a fit when I told him that I wanted his brother private jet painted pink with the words "Berto's World." Roberto and a couple of his other siblings embraced Malice and it was a sight to see. It would take time for Malice to become more open and comfortable with his other siblings like he was with Roberto, but I was proud that my man was even trying.

Roberto was my partner in crime, he put work aside and made time every month to do spa days and just spend time with Malice and I. Killa and Big B were characters as well and even though Malice didn't flat out say it anybody close to our circle could see that Big B and Killa were Malice best friends, they were like brothers to him. When it came to business, Malice was very firm and ran the syndicate with big dick energy.

"I'm staring at the water, damn Malice." I playfully rolled my eyes at his blazing eyes that stayed fixated on me.

"Get up and let's go." I squeezed my thighs together but stood up at his command. This was the part that I loved. Malice loved staying deep inside of me. Every time he slid inside, he would stay inside for the rest of the day or night. He didn't give a damn if his dick was flaccid and all out of nut. He kept that shit inside until it woke back up and he went to work every time.

Malice got behind me and walked me toward our private Villa which was in the center of everyone else's Villa. Each day he had the house butler lay out fresh teal roses just for me to walk on. The roses always led us right to our cozy room.

"We wait until after you have the baby to kill Kenya." He whispered in my ears. I shook my head no.

"That bitch has been sending you letters every damn week. I'm not waiting we leave tomorrow morning and come back here to enjoy the rest of our honeymoon." I was set on killing that bitch. I had no problems with no other females. That Mi'elle chick had gotten married to a ball player.

We ran into Mi'elle at a restaurant with her fiancé two months ago. She tried her hardest to make my man jealous by coming up to our table and inviting us to their wedding. She even let us know that she was pregnant by him. Malice and I both fell out laughing and told the nigga to make sure he made her sign a prenup. Kenya was the opposite; she was still in a mental facility and when she was able to contact people outside of that facility, the first person she called on was Malice.

I was ready to put that bitch out of her misery. She was due to get out of the facility in a couple of days. I had Malice make some calls and already had my medical scrubs and fake badge ready to sneak my way through that bitch to kill her ass.

"Let me find out you got feelings and want to keep her alive." I teased. Malice was in the middle of taking off his boxers and my mouth got watery at the sight of his dick standing up at attention for me.

"Get fucked up, Sove." He gave me a warning glare that didn't move me one bit. Malice loved making fake ass threats that just end up getting me wet.

"Okay then, we leave tomorrow morning. Stick to the plan." It was now my turn to give him my warning glare.

"Bring yo ass here man." He stroked his dick giving me that charming ass sneer that I loved to see. I waddled my pregnant ass right over to my husband and got the dick that I always deserved. The same dick that got me hooked and sprung off a California kingpin!

The End!

NOTE

Small note from Sovereign

I must admit, I'm hooked. I pushed away, and he pulled me back in, then I realized that I'm never pushing away again because he rightfully belongs to me. We are so in tune with one another that it's never hard for us to express and understand each other. Even if I don't say it that nigga knows it. Thought I couldn't even carry a child of my own and he proved me wrong and he's a damn good daddy. Boss ass, big dick freak nigga with a side of crazy that gets this pussy wet as fuck. I did the honors of offing that bitch Kenya Monroe, hate sis had to go out bad like that. A dickmatized woman is worse than a hoe! She had it coming. I knew I made the perfect decision when I walked up into that room of hers and saw her chanting and humming my husband's name, I damn near lost it. She even carved my man's name into her skin and was sitting in a rocking chair staring at his picture. Yea! That part, see what I mean? Off with that dickmatized bitch head. I was no longer a Queenpin, I was a full-time mother that now owned my own skin care company. I'm looking to open up more facilities to help get folks skin together, something I love to do! Thanks for reading my story and be on the lookout for Soulful Hurtz book in the near future! Sovereign ~

STAY CONNECTED

Leave a review on Amazon and tell me what you all think!

Contact the author!

Hey Pieces! It means so much to me to get your honest feedback. Please feel free to join my private readers group on Facebook! **Masterpiece Readers**

Join my mailing list by texting **Masterpiecebooks** *altogether to the number 22828!*

Contact me on any of my social media handles as well!

Facebook- Authoress Masterpiece & Masterpiece Reads

Facebook private group for updates- Masterpiece Readers

Instagram- authoress_masterpiece & masterpiece_lgee

Email – masterpiece3541@outlook.com

Made in United States
Orlando, FL
02 May 2023

32710034R00113